**W9-CFU-248**

Ref

# WANTED: WHITE WEDDING

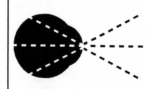

This Large Print Book carries the
Seal of Approval of N.A.V.H.

# WANTED: WHITE WEDDING

## NATASHA OAKLEY

**THORNDIKE PRESS**
*A part of Gale, Cengage Learning*

GALE
CENGAGE Learning™

Detroit • New York • San Francisco • New Haven, Conn • Waterville, Maine • London

GALE
CENGAGE Learning™

**LIBRARY OF CONGRESS CATALOGING-IN-PUBLICATION DATA**

Oakley, Natasha.
    Wanted: white wedding / by Natasha Oakley.
      p. cm. — (Thorndike Press large print core)
    ISBN-13: 978-1-4104-1325-3 (alk. paper)
    ISBN-10: 1-4104-1325-X (alk. paper)
    1. Large type books. I. Title.
PR6115.A38W36 2009
813'.6—dc22
                                      2008043178

Published in 2009 by arrangement with Harlequin Books S.A.

Dear Reader,

As anyone who has visited my blog will know, it's been a very tough time for me and mine. I'm sure that many of you reading this will also have known difficult times. Maybe you're in one of those dark patches right now. And even when life is on an even keel there are still those days when you just feel completely frazzled and worn out, aren't there? It's because life can be tough that I believe time out to read a romance is so very important — one of those little treats that make everything seem more rosy and manageable somehow.

I love writing romance. I get to give my characters real problems and losses — the kind we all face — and then I give them the resolution we all desperately want for ourselves. I believe absolutely that life can change for the better in a moment, and there is nothing better than a "happy ever after."

Thank God for Harlequin Romance® novels.

Much love,
*Natasha*

*To Jenny, my editor.*

*Without your support and belief in me
this book would never have been written.*

*Thank you.*

# CHAPTER ONE

Freya bit down hard on the expletive hovering on the tip of her tongue and called again, her eyes raking the rows of old sofas and chests of drawers. 'Hello?'

There was still no answer. No sound of anything in the cavernous building except the clip of her heels on the concrete floor. 'Mr Ramsay? Anyone? Anyone at all?' She came to a stop and looked back across the auction house.

She sucked in her breath and spun round to look again at the long line of caged cupboards piled high with knick-knacks. Where was everyone? The entire place was deserted.

Freya tucked her hands further into the depths of her sheepskin jacket and stamped her feet to get warmth back into her frozen toes. This was such a crazy way of doing business. There had to be someone whose job it was to speak to people like her. A

9

porter? Wasn't that the way it worked?

She hadn't expected anything like Sotheby's or Christie's in a place like Fellingham, but this was plain ridiculous. Left to herself, she'd walk straight back out of here — and a casual trawl through the telephone directory would, no doubt, produce any number of more promising alternatives.

Except . . .

Her almost habitual frown snapped into place. Except Daniel Ramsay had somehow managed to convince her grandmother he was all things wonderful. *Damn him!*

Twelve years' hard experience had taught her that anyone who gave the appearance of being 'too good to be true' was usually exactly that. The trouble was it would take something approaching the impact of World War Three to shift the elderly woman from her opinion of him now.

Freya pulled her hand out of her pocket and glanced down at her wristwatch. Where was he? She really wanted to see Daniel Ramsay for herself, gauge what kind of man he was, and preferably without her grandmother being there to witness it.

She stepped back, and her leg jagged against a box of china on the floor behind her. She swore softly and bent down to brush the dust off the fine black wool of her trousers.

What kind of place was he running here? Whatever the reality of Daniel Ramsay turned out to be, he was no businessman. His auction house was full of junk. Row upon row of it.

Freya looked round, her nose wrinkled against the musty smell. He couldn't be doing more than scratching a living here . . .

She frowned. No doubt that was why he'd gone out of his way to befriend her grandmother. Stopping to chat and eat lemon drizzle cake whenever he had an hour free.

He'd certainly managed to inveigle himself very successfully. According to her grandmother, his prowess extended from the removal of mice to changing a lightbulb. And, of course, antiques. Apparently Daniel Ramsay knew *everything* there was to know about antiques . . .

Freya stamped her foot again as the cold bit at her toes. Looking at the sad specimens around her, she seriously doubted that. In her opinion his 'gift', such as it was, was in correctly reading an elderly woman who wanted shot of things she didn't much value but which he knew would earn him a hefty commission.

Her eyes fixed on the green painted door with the small 'Office' sign on it. She gave her wristwatch another swift glance and then sidestepped the box, pushing her way passed a battered rocking horse.

This was a stupid waste of her time. If the office door was unlocked she'd leave a note, asking him to call this afternoon.

Not perfect. Not what she'd hoped for. But better than nothing. And it was always possible she was worrying needlessly anyway. Perhaps Daniel Ramsay genuinely liked spending time with her grandmother and had no ulterior motive at all?

Only. . . .

Freya's eyes narrowed as her normal scepticism rose to the surface. Only that wasn't very likely. Not in the least likely. She rapped with her knuckles on the closed office door, scarcely pausing before pushing it open. 'Mr Rams . . . ?'

His name died on her lips as she took in the threadbare rug and the muddle of . . . stuff. There was no other word to describe the eclectic mix of furniture and paintings. All of which would have been better consigned to a skip rather than an auction house.

What was going on here? Was this some kind of 'lost and found'? Or a modern-day 'rag and bone' business?

She picked her way across the floor and

stopped by the heavy oak desk, one part of her mind speculating how anyone could work in such disorder while the other questioned whether the elusive Daniel Ramsay would even be able to find a note left for him in the mess.

Freya let out her breath on a slow, steady stream and pulled her handbag from her shoulder. She set it on the desk, starting slightly as the telephone on the other side of it started to ring. Conditioned as she was to take all her calls within a few seconds, it set her teeth on edge to hear it echo off into the distance via a crude tannoy system.

She reached across to pull a pen from a colourful mug, starting as the office door banged violently against the wall.

'Get that, will you?'

'I'm —'

'The phone. Take a message,' a disembodied male voice shouted, followed by a grunt. 'I'll be through in a minute.'

'I —'

'Phone! Just answer the phone!'

For a brief second she wondered whether she'd inadvertently stepped into a farce, and then Freya shrugged, stepping over a pile of vinyl records and an old gramophone to reach the other side of the desk. What did it matter? And at least it would stop that infernal noise ricocheting about.

'Ramsay Auctioneers,' she said into the receiver, her eyes on the closed door.

'Daniel? Is that you?'

Hardly. She rubbed a hand across her eyes, the humour of the situation finally reaching her. 'I'm sorry, Mr Ramsay isn't available at the moment. May I take a message?'

'Can you tell him Tom Hamber called, love?'

Her right eyebrow flicked up and she reached over the scattered papers for a pad of fluorescent sticky notes. In her real life she'd have paused to tell Tom Hamber she wasn't his 'love'. She might even have told him that while she *could* pass on a message, she was by no means certain she would . . .

'Have you got that? You won't forget?'

'Tom Hamber called,' she said dryly, drawing a box around the words she'd written. 'I think I'll manage to remember.'

'Tell him I need to speak to him before midday.'

Freya added the words 'before midday' to the note, then turned at the sound of a loud crash. 'I'll leave him a note,' she said into the receiver. Whether he actually found it really wasn't her problem.

'That's it, love.'

She set the receiver back on its cradle, ripping the top note off the pile. One thing she was certain of: there was no way on earth she was going to let her grandmother sell anything valuable through this crazy set-up. She looked at the confusion on the desk and stuck the note firmly on the telephone.

'Thanks for that.'

Freya turned and found she was looking up into a pair of brown eyes. Very definitely up. At five feet ten — more in heels — it wasn't often she had to do that.

*Why did that feel so good?* Some deep Freudian something was probably at the root of it. He had to be at least six foot two. Quite possibly more. And those eyes . . . Dark, *dark* brown, and sexy beyond belief.

'I was holding up one end of a table and couldn't let go.'

Freya pulled her eyes away from his and wrapped her sheepskin jacket closely around her. 'Right.'

'Did you get a message?'

'Yes. Y-yes, I did. Yes.' The corner of his mouth quirked and she stumbled on, feeling as foolish as if she'd been caught drooling. 'It was a Tom Hamber.'

'Ah.'

'He wants to speak to Daniel Ramsay before midday.'

15

'I can do that.'

The most horrible suspicion darted into her head.

'I'm Daniel Ramsay.' He smiled, and Freya felt as though the floor had disappeared beneath her.

*This* couldn't be Daniel Ramsay. From her grandmother's conversation she'd conjured up a very different picture. Someone altogether more parochial. More . . .

Well . . . less, if she were honest. Much less. Truthfully, this Daniel Ramsay looked like the kind of man you'd quite like to wake up with on a lazy Sunday morning. A little bit rumpled and a whole lot sexy.

'You're a little late.' Then he smiled again, wiping his hands on the back of dark blue denim jeans, and the effect was intensified. 'Not to worry. I get here about eight thirty, but I told the agency nine-thirty was fine.'

He held out a hand, and she automatically held out her own. His wedding ring flashed. *Of course* a man who looked like this one would be taken. They always were — even if they pretended not to be.

A familiar sense of dissatisfaction speared her. It was amazing how many men said they were separated when the only thing keeping them apart from their significant other was temporary geographical distance.

She was so tired of that. Tired of the game-playing.

Daniel bent down and pulled open the bottom drawer of his desk. 'I've got the key to the inner office here. I'll show you where everything is, and then I've got to drive out to the Penry-James farm.'

'I'm not —'

He stood straight. 'Which part didn't you get?'

'I understood you perfectly, but I'm not from any agency.'

'You're not?'

'Merely a potential customer.'

His hand raked through his dark hair. 'Hell, I'm so sorry! I thought —'

'I was someone else.' It didn't take the mental agility of Einstein to figure that one out. It was vaguely reassuring to know he didn't actively intend to run his business in such a haphazard way.

Sudden laughter lit his eyes, and she fought against the curl of attraction deep in her abdomen.

'So you're not the cavalry after all? Perhaps we'd better start over?'

'Perhaps,' she murmured, feeling unaccountably strange as his hand wrapped round hers for the second time. He had nice hands, she registered. Strong, with neatly cut nails. And a voice that made her feel as though she'd stepped into a vat of chocolate.

But *taken,* the logical part of her brain reminded her. And apparently the kind of man who, if he wasn't actually preying on her grandmother, was certainly making the most of an opportunity.

'You must have thought I was mad. Did Tom say what he wanted?'

'No, he didn't.'

'I expect it's about the quiz night next month.' His smile widened and her stomach flipped over. Helplessly. 'So, if you're not from the agency, what can I do for you?'

'Not me. My grandmother,' she said, her voice unnecessarily clipped as she struggled to regain her usual control.

She took a deep breath and exhaled in one slow, steady stream, watching the droplets hang in the frosty air. 'Is it always this cold in here?'

'Not in summer.' He moved away and bent to switch on a fan heater. 'Then it can get quite unpleasant —'

'It's unpleasant now!'

He looked up, his brown eyes glinting with sexy laughter. 'Because the window in here doesn't open,' he continued, as though she hadn't spoken, completely unfazed. 'It's been painted over too many times.'

18

She bit back the observation that getting a window to open was something which could be easily fixed. Something that most certainly would be in any sensibly run business.

'I suppose I ought to sort that.'

'I would.'

He gave a bark of laughter. Startled, Freya looked at him. It had been a long, long time since anyone had dared laugh at her. She took in the faint amber flecks in his laughing eyes and swallowed, desperately willing her throat to work normally.

He was so entirely unexpected. She'd got one image of him entrenched so firmly in her imagination that this incarnation was difficult to adjust to. She tucked a strand of hair behind her left ear and felt the back of her hand brush against her crystal earring. It started swinging and jagged against the collar of her jacket.

'How can I help your grandmother?'

Freya blinked. 'She has a few items she's interested in selling, and I'd like to have a professional evaluation of them.'

'Can you bring them in?'

'Not easily. There's a chiffonier, a dining table —'

'Then I'll come out to her.' He moved effortlessly past the piled boxes and sat

19

behind his heavy desk, taking a pen from the same chipped mug she had.

'Today, if possible.'

He nodded, his pen poised. 'And you are?'

Freya hesitated. She wasn't quite ready to tell him that. Not exactly, anyway. Three days in Fellingham and she'd already had more than enough of people's reaction to her name. From the way their eyebrows shot up into their scalp she could only assume she'd gone down in local folklore as all things depraved.

It shouldn't matter. Didn't. But somewhere not so deeply buried her anger about that was still there. Nibbling away at her, despite all the success which had followed.

'My grandmother's Margaret Anthony. Mrs Margaret Anthony.'

His sexy eyes narrowed slightly. If she hadn't been so attuned to people's reaction to her she'd probably have missed it. Possibly even the beat of silence which followed. 'Then that would make you Freya Anthony.'

'That's right.'

His strong fingers opened a large black diary and he wrote her grandmother's name at the end of a long list. 'It looks like it'll have to be near five. I'm a little choked up today.'

'That's fine.'

He looked up and his eyes were no longer laughing. Something inside her withered a little more. He was a stranger to her, an 'incomer' to the area, and yet he'd already formed a poor opinion of her.

But then of course he had. What was she thinking? She knew Fellingham's vicious network had gone into overdrive, and it didn't take much imagination to guess what he must have heard about her.

'Has she thought any more about selling her vases?'

'She's thought about it.'

'And?'

Freya held his gaze, meaning to intimidate. She could do that. She'd always been able to do that. 'I'm going to make sure she gets the best possible price for them. I understand an undamaged pair can be quite valuable.'

'Can be. You just need two collectors who badly want to own them.' Daniel stood up. 'I think she could confidently expect to get a thousand for them.'

'And in London?'

He shrugged, completely unfazed by the question she'd shot at him. 'Possibly more. But the internet is narrowing the gap. Dedicated collectors search online.'

'I wasn't aware you had much of a web-site here.'

'It's in development.'

'But very early stages,' she said dismiss-ively. 'So not much use yet.' Freya lifted her jacket collar and snuggled down into the warmth.

It didn't matter what he thought of her. The only thing that mattered was her grandmother, and she was going to do anything and everything to see she wasn't hurt or cheated. Not by him or anyone. 'I'll tell my grandmother to expect you.'

Daniel nodded. 'As near to five as I can make it.'

'We'll both be there.' She gave him a swift smile, one that didn't quite reach her eyes, before picking up her bag and walking out of the office.

# CHAPTER TWO

So that was the notorious Ms Anthony. Daniel watched the swing of her hips as she left . . . because he couldn't help it. She had the longest legs. The kind that would wrap around you twice. Then he listened to the sound of her ridiculous heels clipping on the concrete floor until it faded to nothing. He shoved his hands deep in his jeans pockets.

Not exactly what he'd been expecting Fellingham's very own bad girl to be like. *Interesting.*

He carelessly tossed his pen back into the orange and red mug. Freya was a great name for her, though. If he'd ever taken a moment to think about it, he'd have thought someone who was named after the Scandinavian goddess of love and beauty ought to look pretty much like she did.

Daniel fingered the tag on the Gabrielle cream plush Paddington Bear that was destined for the twentieth century sale later in the month. Margaret Stone's wayward granddaughter would need to be beautiful to have lived one fraction of the life village gossip attributed to her.

He hadn't expected her to so obviously exude class, though. Hell only knew why not. He'd known all about her Audi Roadster within minutes of it driving into the village. He shouldn't have been surprised by the skilfully highlighted blond hair and the designer clothes.

'Dan?'

He turned.

'We've got a problem.' His porter rested his hand on the doorframe. 'The blonde bombshell wants Pete's van moved. It's blocking her car in.'

'Damn!'

'She's being quite vocal about it.'

'I just bet.'

The porter gave a rare grin. 'I told her the driver had gone for breakfast and wouldn't be back for twenty minutes or so, but she's not having none of that. Says my time might be worthless but hers isn't. She wants it moved right now.'

Somehow he didn't find it difficult to accept that Freya Anthony expected things to happen when and where she wanted. One imperious click of her manicured fingers and Daniel had no doubt the world habitually fell where she wanted it to.

'I'll talk to her.'

'You'll have to. She's spitting fair to blow.'

Daniel smiled. The image Bob was creating was all too indicative of what he expected Ms Anthony would do when the world didn't bend to her will.

'She's one that likes things to happen yesterday, I reckon.'

'Okay, I'll sort it.' Daniel glanced down at his watch and grimaced. There couldn't be much more that could go wrong today. He seemed to have been running behind from the minute he'd opened his eyes this morning.

'Nice looking woman, though, ain't she?'

Yes — if you liked the kind of woman who would eat you up and spit you out.

He stepped out onto the forecourt, pausing for a minute to gauge how blocked-in her car was. The faint hope he'd had that it might be possible to guide her past faded as he took in how far Pete had driven the van in.

Daniel walked towards her. 'I'm sorry about this.'

'Just get it moved.'

He looked back at Bob. 'See if you can

find Pete and get the keys —'

'You don't have a spare set?'

'Why would I? It's not my van,' he replied calmly, taking in the angry flash of her blue eyes. Then he turned back to Bob. 'I think you'll find him in Carlo's. If not he'll have gone on to that place in the arcade for one of their all-day breakfasts.'

The older man nodded and ambled off towards Silver Street. Beside him, Freya made a small guttural sound of pure irritation.

'It shouldn't be too long,' Daniel offered. 'Would you like to wait inside?'

'What's the difference? It's as cold in there as out here.'

'You're welcome to use the phone if you need to call someone,' he added seamlessly.

'I've got a mobile.'

Quite deliberately he let the silence stretch out between them. She could be as difficult as she liked, but she wasn't going to get a reaction out of him. After a moment it seemed she made a conscious decision to relax. Though by other people's standards she was still as tense as a bowstring.

Spoilt, he thought, watching the small frown disappear from the centre of her forehead. A woman who'd had her own way far too often and easily. She spun round on her ice-pick-thin heels and walked over to perch half a buttock on the low brick wall behind her car.

His eyes travelled to the sleek grey Audi he'd heard so much about. 'Nice car.'

'I like it.'

Daniel smiled. It was a 'statement' car, not one chosen simply to get you from A to B. It was a car which would always be noticed. Would inspire envy. She had to know that. Would surely have anticipated the reaction it would produce when she drove it into the village. Even in Fellingham, which had its fair share of London money.

It made him wonder whether this was all some kind of game to her. Did she like the idea of wafting back to her old stamping ground and giving the gossips something to talk about?

Because they *were* talking. Everything she did and said would be dissected. Everywhere she went . . .

Did she even care?

Daniel took in the dark smudges under her eyes and the tight hold to her mouth. She cared. He had no idea how he knew that so certainly. 'How long are you planning on staying?'

'I've not decided.'

'Nice to have the freedom to choose.' Daniel sat down on the wall beside her, perversely determined to make her speak. 'Is Margaret still planning on moving to a warden-controlled place?'

He was aware of the slight hunch to her shoulders and the short delay before she replied. 'Quite possibly.' Then, 'You know, you really don't need to wait with me.'

'It's not a problem.'

'I'm sure —' She broke off with a swift frown. '*Bob,* was it?'

Daniel nodded.

'Well, I'm sure Bob will manage to find the driver of that thing,' she said, pointing at the white van, 'and get it moved some time before lunch. You go on doing whatever it is you need to do.'

Daniel stretched out his legs. 'Pete's on his break, so you're going to need me to reverse it. Unless . . . you're happy to do it yourself?'

'I've no problem with that.'

He fought down an unexpected desire to laugh. She'd do it. A vehicle she didn't know, and a tight bend out on to a narrow road . . .

He'd kind of like to see that. It was a shame Bob would refuse to hand over the keys. Pete would have him lynched if there

28

was even the slightest scratch put on his baby.

'Pete might have a problem with it. That's his pride and joy.'

'Then why make the suggestion?'

Fair question. Why had he? Daniel studied her face for a moment.

Because he liked to see the challenging tilt of her chin, the determination in a face that otherwise looked as if it could be the model for a porcelain doll . . .

Freya Anthony had the darkest lashes of any woman he'd ever seen. Though maybe they looked like that because her skin was so fair. Purple smudges beneath blue eyes. Intelligent eyes. Guarded.

Hurt.

He recognised that because he'd felt it. There was always an unspoken connection between people who knew what it was to suffer.

Daniel shook his head. An affinity between two souls who knew life wasn't perfect. Could never be perfect. And for some reason he knew this carefully packaged blonde understood that. She knew it with the same bone-deep certainty he did.

'If we're going to be sitting here a while, shall I bring us out a couple of coffees?'

'No.' Then, as though some semblance of

politeness was dragged out of her, 'I'm not thirsty, but that's no reason for you not to go and get one for yourself if you're determined to babysit me.' She stood up and tapped her foot against the tarmac.

Daniel's eyes travelled to the caramel suede of her boot, the impatient movement of her foot. 'No problem. I'll just sit here and wait with you.'

'How long have you known my grandmother?'

The question surprised him. Or rather the antagonistic tone of it did. He shrugged. 'A few years —'

'How come?'

His eyes moved back up to her face, taking in the pinched look. Daniel sat back as far as the wall would allow. *What exactly was her problem?* Something had really got under her skin. And that something appeared to be him.

Maybe she was the possessive sort? Perhaps she wasn't happy to discover Margaret had filled the void left by her family, if not well at least adequately?

'Margaret takes an interest in other people's lives,' he said slowly. 'People like her for it.' He watched her process that — make some kind of judgement. Her foot moved again, and she spun round so he couldn't see her face.

'How much longer is this Bob going to be? This is completely stupid.'

'That'll depend on how difficult Pete's been to find.'

Her head snapped round, her long earrings swinging. 'I've got things I need to be doing.'

Daniel felt a smile twitch at the side of his mouth. Unreasonable and spoilt was the only way to describe Freya Anthony's behaviour.

Very similar, in fact, to the way his daughter behaved when he vetoed something or other 'everyone else' was doing. Only Mia was fifteen, and had considerably more excuse for behaving like a brat than a woman in her late twenties . . . however beautiful.

*Oh, hell!* The thought of his daughter had him reaching inside his coat pocket for his phone. He'd forgotten to turn it back on, which meant her school wouldn't have been able to contact him if . . .

What did he mean *if* they tried to call? Given the morning they'd had, it was an inevitability. It was a little over three years since Anna had died, and he'd never missed his wife as much as he did right now.

Anna would have known what to do.

She'd have had one of those mother/ daughter chats the 'How to Deal with your Teenager' books suggested.

*But Mia might not have been behaving the way she was if Anna hadn't died . . .* Daniel closed his eyes against the thought. Things were the way they were. They just had to be got through in the best way possible.

It wasn't what he'd have chosen. None of it was as he'd chosen —

A bleep alerted him to a missed call. Damn it!

He looked up, and Freya waved an impatient hand towards him. A fatalistic sense of foreboding settled on him as he pushed the button that would let him hear the message. It was brief, and very much to the point. Daniel pulled a hand across the back of his neck.

'Trouble?'

He turned. 'I need to make a call.' Cold wind whipped at the fine blonde hair she'd loosely clipped up. He shouldn't really leave her sitting here alone, waiting for goodness only knew how long. Daniel hesitated before his priorities slipped into their habitual pattern. 'I'm sorry, I really do —'

'It's fine.'

His hand bounced his phone. 'It's my daughter's school —'

'It's fine,' she repeated, and for the first time her eyes lost their hard, combative edge.

It was so dramatic a change that it cut through his preoccupation.

'If I have to wait for Pete to finish his break, then that's what I'll have to do.'

Daniel studied her eyes, looking for some kind of explanation for such an abrupt change of manner. 'I'll —'

'See you at five,' she finished for him, returning to sit uncomfortably on the wall.

'Thank you. I really appreciate that.'

Freya climbed into the driver's seat and leant across to reach into the glove compartment of her car, pulling out some lip balm.

*She hadn't done that well.* Any of it. Not only had she not really been able to gauge what sort of man Daniel Ramsay was, she'd probably done more harm than good. After witnessing her behaviour today, he probably thought her grandmother needed protection from *her.*

Nothing about this visit was going as she'd planned. She unclipped the twisted silver barrette, throwing it on the passenger seat, and ran her fingers through her hair. What exactly was she so cross about anyway?

For all she knew Daniel Ramsay was a

genuinely kind man, trying to make a go of a small country auction house. He'd seemed kind. After all, how many men in her London circle would drop everything to go running when their daughter's school rang?

That didn't take very much thinking about. None. She didn't know anyone like that.

She shut the glove compartment with a hard shove. It was the fault of this wretched place. She couldn't seem to stop herself from behaving badly. Maybe because that was what everyone was expecting from her? Who knew what the psychology was? Whatever it was, she was certainly living down to their expectations.

Steve, the driver of the white van, walked past her car, sparing her only the briefest of glances. No doubt this morning's performance would be added to the canon of her supposed misdemeanours. Only in this case she was more than a little guilty.

Freya bit her lip. Why had she ever thought coming back here was a good idea? Okay, so she'd thought her physical presence might deter her dad more effectively than the knowledge she was watching from a distance, but there was more to it than that.

So many complex reasons bound up together. The fact was, this whole approaching thirty thing had taken on a life of itself. It felt almost like a life crisis. At least it would if she didn't hope to live considerably longer than sixty years.

Now she had something to prove — to herself if no one else. She *would not* run back to London like a dog with its tail between its legs simply because other people didn't like her. Been there, done that, had the battle scars to prove it.

But being back in Fellingham did make her feel as judged as before. And after twelve years she honestly hadn't expected it to feel like that. She could feel everything unravelling. All her hard-won peace of mind.

Statements like *It's so important to feel no residual anger towards anyone or anything* no longer seemed to make sense. What did it mean when you actually unpicked it?

She was angry — *really* angry. How about *One's past must not be allowed to determine one's future?* Wasn't that what her therapist had said?

It was all total rubbish. Freya turned the key in the ignition. Clearly Dr Stefanie Coxan had no first-hand knowledge of what it was like to live in a gossipy little place like Fellingham.

Of *course* one's past shaped one's future. Even if you managed to draw a black line under the grotty bits, pieces of it still steeped through and stained whatever came after.

She reversed out into the narrow country lane and, without stopping to analyse why, turned her car towards Kilbury. Post-war bungalows still lined the entrance to the village, followed by a rash of 1930s semis, many carefully extended beyond recognition.

She took the left-hand turn towards Church Lane, the second right into Wood End Road, and bit down a wave of pure loathing as Kilbury Comprehensive School appeared from behind a row of Leylandi.

Squat. Ugly. Built of breeze blocks some time in the 1970s, when it had seemed a good idea to make everything square and functional. She slowed her car down to a stop as large droplets of rain spotted the windscreen.

There'd been nowhere on earth she'd been more unhappy. Nothing to do with the school, of course. Now, with hindsight, she could see that. Everything that had tortured her had been from within. But at the time it had been just another thing to kick against. Something else to resent.

Freya glanced down at her watch and restarted the engine. There was no point in sitting here remembering how unhappy she'd been. If she'd hoped seeing it again would lay some ghosts to rest she'd been kidding herself. If anything it felt as if she'd stirred a few up.

Freya turned the car round in a lay-by and headed back along the main road towards Fellingham. She set her windscreen wipers going and flicked on her headlights to compensate for the overall gloom.

It was strange to be driving along this road. It was all so familiar, and yet not. The red telephone box had been replaced by one of those see-through boxes. The pub at the end of the lane had changed from the Pheasant to the Plough.

But most things were the same.

Presumably the school bus still took this route. Still left at 7:25 a.m. from the bus stop opposite the garage, still took a lengthy detour through Westbury and Levingham before looping round to Kilbury.

She slowed at the crossroads and glanced over at the brick-built bus shelter which had been her escape route. It hadn't taken too much ingenuity to slip out through the changing rooms, cross behind the bike sheds and then walk down the main road to this bus stop. From there it had been a twenty-minute ride into Olban and all the diversions of a big town.

And it seemed times hadn't changed much. Out of the corner of her eye she caught sight of a teenage girl in school uniform, turning away from the wind to light a cigarette.

As she pulled away from Pelham Forest it crossed her mind to wonder whether she should have stopped. But then what would she have done? Or said?

You couldn't just pick up stray adolescents. There were laws against that type of thing. And if that girl was anything like she'd been at the same age she'd have given her a mouthful for interfering in what didn't concern her.

But . . .

Freya glanced in her rearview mirror, softly biting her lip. *Maybe she ought to ring the school?* She debated with herself for all of thirty seconds. She couldn't do it. It would feel like a betrayal. *Honour among thieves, and all that.*

From the distance she heard the slow rumble of thunder. Moments later there was a crack of lightning.

Freya glanced again in her rearview mirror but she'd driven on too far to be able to see what the teenager's reaction to the storm was. It was one hell of a day to have picked to bunk off school.

It was all too easy for her to imagine how that girl must be feeling. And how cold. Freya swore softly and steeled herself to go back and check the teenager was at least okay.

At the next junction she performed an illegal U-turn and drove back up the other way. It was one thing not to want to deliberately get someone into trouble, quite another to drive off leaving them wet and miserable.

The light from her headlights picked up the rain, now coming down like stair-rods. Despite it, the girl stepped straight out and lifted her thumb — which certainly made it all much easier. Freya gave quiet thanks that she didn't have to get out of the car. She slowed and came to a stop.

'You in trouble?' she asked, opening the window with the push of a button.

'The bus is late and I've got an appointment in Olban.' The girl took a drag on her cigarette. 'Are you going that way? I could use a lift.'

Rain slipped in through the opened window, darkening the suede of Freya's jacket. One glance at the teenager showed she was faring much worse. Her khaki coat was sodden, and her hair, dragged back in a tight ponytail, hung limply down the back of her neck.

'What time's your appointment?' Freya asked, mentally reviewing her options. Now she was here she wasn't at all sure what she was going to do.

'Twelve-fifteen. I'm meeting my mum at McDonalds.'

*And she believed that just about as much as she wanted a hole in the head.* 'Can I ring her? To check she doesn't mind me giving you a lift?'

'She won't mind.'

'I'd like to ring her anyway.'

'My phone's died,' she said, with a jut to her chin, then brushed a long strand of sodden hair off her cheek.

'We can use mine.'

'I can't remember her number.'

Freya's hands moved over the steering wheel. *Hell,* this kind of thing never happened to her in London. For one thing she was always too busy to notice if anyone was out of place.

*Damn it!* She really should have just rung the school. They could have checked their records and she could have driven back to Fellingham guilt free.

'Are you going to take me?' The girl took another drag on her cigarette and then dropped it to the ground, twisting the ball of her foot on it. 'I won't smoke in your car. And I've got a plastic bag in here,' she said, lifting her schoolbag forward. 'I can lay it across the seat if you're worried about your leather.'

Freya fought the smile that tugged at the corner of her mouth. This girl was only a beginner in delinquency. Way back when, she wouldn't have said anything like that. She'd have been more inclined to smoke if she thought it would shock, and the idea of protecting a car seat just wouldn't have occurred to her.

'I can give you a lift, but I need to ring your school and ask them to contact your mum. I need her permission.'

'Don't bother.' The girl turned back towards the shelter, her shoulders braced against the wind.

'You know hitch-hiking is dangerous,' Freya offered, wincing at words she knew would achieve nothing. 'I might be anyone.'

The girl looked over her shoulder. 'But you're not. You're Freya Anthony. I've seen you before.'

'Have you?'

'And everyone's talking about you.'

*Ah.* Why did that still have the power to surprise her? 'Do I get to know *your* name?'

'Do I get a lift?' she countered.

It was a little like looking into a mirror. Albeit one that had the ability to turn back time. There was something else, too. Some sense that she'd seen this girl somewhere before. Maybe it was nothing more than the ghosts of her youth haunting her. Reminding her.

'It's pouring down out here, and I'm wet.'

'I . . .' Freya was momentarily distracted by a bright light shining in her rearview mirror. She looked up and then over her shoulder as a silver estate car bore done on her.

The girl swore, and Freya turned in time to see her duck out of sight. *What the — ?*

The lights were switched off and a car door slammed behind her. Freya swung round in her seat and she watched, amazed, as Daniel Ramsay stormed over towards the shelter.

*Oh . . . my . . . goodness.* She made the connection surprisingly slowly. Somehow it had never occurred to her that a man the age of Daniel Ramsay would have a daughter as old as this one. But that had to be it. Every line of his body screamed his anger.

His dark eyes met hers briefly, but his attention was on the belligerent teenager. Fascinated, she watched the confident, mouthy girl turn into a sulky, quiet one.

Freya deliberately looked away, and carefully re-zipped the inner pocket of her handbag.

She felt a strange pang of envy watching the two of them. No one had ever come looking for her. Certainly not her dad. Not ever. It would have meant a lot if he had. If just once he'd put her first. Freya brushed an irritated hand across her eyes. It had been such a long time since she'd allowed herself to be so affected by thoughts like that. It didn't matter.

Not any more.

*Her parents were her parents. They'd done the best they could and that was that. One's worth must come from inside oneself.* She only wished she could believe that . . . on some level other than a cerebral one.

'Ms Anthony?'

Freya looked up.

'Is that yours or hers?' he asked abruptly, his voice edged with anger and his eyes on the cigarette butt on the kerb.

'I'm sorry?'

'The cigarette?'

His voice was like steel . . . and she instinctively reacted against it. *Who did he think he was, to be talking to her like that?* She glanced at his daughter, standing sullenly behind him, and caught the appeal for help in her eyes. It was fleeting. Barely there before it was gone. And Freya couldn't do anything but respond to the sense of kinship she felt.

'You have a problem with that?'

His brown eyes narrowed infinitesimally. 'Actually, plenty. But if you want to sabotage your chances of living into old age so be it.' He turned his head. 'Mia, get in the car. Now. I said *now!*'

The teenager allowed herself a quick glance of gratitude towards Freya before doing as she was told. It was amazing how much 'attitude' she still managed to exude. Even the slam of the door spoke volumes.

Freya turned back to look at Mia's father, feeling a little guilty.

He took a moment, seemingly trying to gain some control. 'That wasn't helpful. I don't know what you think you're playing at, but —'

'I —'

'— if she'd actually got into your car I'd have seriously considered charging you with abduction.'

'I —'

'I suggest, in future, you mind your own business,' he said, stepping back from her car and heading towards his own.

Freya sat, a little stunned at his attack.

She felt as though she'd been verbally cut off at the knees. And people said *she* had a tongue dipped in vitriol.

She wouldn't care to be in Mia's shoes right now, she thought as she caught a glimpse of Daniel's expression as he drove past. There was a price to being loved, it seemed. Because she didn't doubt he was motivated by that.

Even so . . . he'd had no business talking to her like that. Slowly she reached down for the ignition to start the engine.

Surely it had been a tad disproportionate? She'd known from his reaction to her name earlier that he'd heard something of her history, but what exactly did he think she'd want with a truanting teenager? Did he honestly imagine she went around the country finding disaffected girls to turn into mini versions of her?

After starting the engine, Freya pulled away from the kerb. The sooner she got out of this spiteful little place the happier she'd be.

# CHAPTER THREE

'Is your granddaughter here?' Daniel asked, shaking the rain from his coat. 'I'd like a word with her if I may?'

'Through there.' Margaret nodded towards the door to the dining room. 'I don't think you're Freya's favourite person right now.'

'I don't imagine I am. May I — ?'

'Go through,' she said with a smile, giving every appearance of thoroughly enjoying herself. 'I'll put on the kettle. Call if you need rescuing.'

Daniel walked down the hallway, but he didn't venture further than the doorway. Freya was there. Wrapping china and seemingly absorbed in her task.

He stood with one hand on the doorjamb, searching for the words he knew he needed to say — and trying to whip up some anger towards Mia for having placed him in this embarrassing situation.

*But he knew this was about him.* He'd spent long enough over the past few months talking about personal responsibility to know he'd no one to blame but himself for the way he'd spoken to Freya.

He'd done it because he could, he supposed. Because he'd needed someone to blame. Someone to take out his anger and frustration on.

Only . . .

Only — and this was the damnable part — he'd seen the slight widening of her blue eyes and caught the hurt in them. A fleeting expression. Swiftly controlled. But he'd seen it — and it felt as he imagined he would feel if he kicked a puppy.

There were enough people round and about who were ready to stick the knife into Freya Anthony, and he didn't intend to be one of them. She was here now. That was wonderful, as far as Margaret was concerned, and if she was happy he had no business making it hard for her granddaughter to stay.

Which meant he had to put things right.

*Try to.* This wasn't going to be easy. The slight tilt of her head told him Freya knew he was there, but that she'd no intention of meeting him halfway.

And why should she? He thrust his right

hand deep in his jeans pocket. 'I owe you an apology.'

Freya looked up momentarily from the bubble-wrap she was cutting. 'Yes, you do.' She reached for the top saucer from a pile to her left and placed it carefully in the centre of the bubble-wrap.

'What I said to you . . .'

One perfectly shaped eyebrow flicked upwards.

'. . . was . . . was out of line, and I apologise. I was unfair . . . and . . .'

'Rude?' she offered, her voice like a shiver.

*Yes, damn it!* He'd been rude. Completely unreasonable. Daniel pulled his hand out of his pocket and thrust it through his hair. 'I took my anger out on you and I'm sorry. I had no right to do that.'

He'd done it. Made his apology. The best he could do without going into his relationship with his daughter.

'No.'

His mind stuttered. No, his apology wasn't accepted? Or no —

'No right,' she clarified, her fingers moving for a second saucer. 'Would you pass me the sticky tape, please?'

Daniel walked further into the room and picked it up from the far end of the dining table. Stepping closer to her, he caught the waft of her perfume, light and citrus. Saw the pulse beating at the base of her neck . . .

And suddenly it mattered, really mattered, that she should believe him. He'd hurt her, and he had the uncanny sense that far too many people had done that.

He kept hold of the sticky tape as she reached for it and forced her to look up at him. 'I'd like to have shouted at Mia, and since I couldn't I took out my anger on you. Made you my whipping boy, if you like.' His mouth twisted into a wry smile as he saw the flicker of understanding. 'I really am sorry for the way I spoke to you.'

There was a moment's hesitation, then, 'I know that.'

Just three words, but her voice had lost its hard edge, and the underlying huskiness of it seemed to hold him frozen. A small tug on the roll of sticky tape pulled him back to the present. He swallowed, watching as she ripped off a few centimetres and taped it across the top of the pile.

'I can understand why you were angry. I just don't think I deserved —'

'No, you didn't.' *She really didn't.*

She moistened her lips. 'What happened to . . . Mia? Did you get her back to school?'

Freya's concern merely added to his confusion about her. People asked about his

49

daughter all the time, but none of them managed to imbue it with real concern. Why would she care? By all accounts empathy wasn't one of her strong suits, and she'd not been anywhere near Margaret all the time he'd lived in Fellingham. She had to know her grandmother had desperately wanted her to.

'Do you mind my asking?'

'No. No, not at all. I drove her straight there.' Daniel watched as Freya carefully folded over the end of the Sellotape and replaced it on the dining table.

He'd love to know what had made Freya visit now. She didn't look like someone who'd want to spend days on end packing up someone else's possessions. Maybe Sophy was right in thinking she had nowhere else to go?

Her hands moved to cocoon another teacup in bubble-wrap. She made even that mundane task seem faintly exotic. As was her dress ring. Whilst the thumb ring she wore was more bohemian. And she had tiny wrists that reminded him of Anna's.

But that was where the similarities stopped. He looked up at Freya's oval face, with her perfectly shaped eyebrows and carefully accentuated lip colour. The two women couldn't have been more different.

His Anna had been a woman without artifice, whereas Freya couldn't have exerted more care over her appearance. She was beautiful, but he fancied she'd look more beautiful first thing in the morning — before she'd hidden herself away behind her make-up.

He stopped. Maybe she *was* hiding. Maybe that was *exactly* what she was doing. Maybe Freya Anthony was less spoiled and more scared.

God only knew why that bothered him so much. She was nothing to him. But . . .

There'd been something unpleasant about the gossip swirling around the village over the last few days. Something in it he didn't like.

'The school picked up on her absence very quickly,' Freya remarked, placing the saucers into a cardboard box by the wall. 'That was good.'

Daniel put his hands deep in his jeans pockets and determinedly focused on her question. 'They register her at the start of each lesson.' She glanced up at him and he added, 'Unusual, I know, but Mia skips off so often we've got a fairly established routine going now.'

'Is she being bullied?'

'Nothing like that.' *If only it were that*

*simple.* 'There's no real reason. At least not one she's prepared to tell us about. We've got an excellent Educational Welfare Officer assigned to us now, but nothing anyone says to Mia seems to make any difference. She can't see the point of school and that's that.'

'Tea?' Margaret said, coming in behind him with a tray.

Daniel turned to take the tray from her, and she sat herself down in the nearest chair with something like a sigh. 'My hip . . . The sooner I get that operation the better.'

'If you'd go private,' Freya said, rolling the bubble-wrap back on the roll and standing it in the corner, 'you wouldn't have to wait. I keep telling you that.'

'I'm not paying.'

'You wouldn't have to. I would.'

Daniel set the tray on the table as another preconception bit the dust. From everything he'd heard he hadn't expected there to be any kind of emotional connection between Margaret and her granddaughter . . . but there undoubtedly was.

*How come?* Freya Anthony had shaken the Fellingham dust from her shoes a long time ago, and hadn't looked back. Before that she'd been nothing but trouble. But what he was watching wasn't a new reconciliation. There was familiarity in the way they talked to each other. Love.

'I've paid into the National Health Service for nearly fifty years, and I don't see why I should have to pay extra now.'

Freya sat down opposite Margaret, but her blue eyes flicked over in his direction as she picked up the milk jug. 'I assume you take milk?'

'I do. Thank you.'

She poured some in the bone china teacup, and then lifted the matching teapot, steadying the lid with her finger. 'We've been arguing about this for months, and I don't think we're ever going to agree.'

'No, we aren't!'

'It's crazy to go on in pain when there's an alternative.' She passed across her grandmother's tea. 'Just think — when you've had your operation you might not feel the same need to move from here —'

'No one will want this place after I'm gone,' Margaret said, setting the cup down in front of her and reaching for the sugar bowl. 'This is a family home. I should have sold it a long time ago.'

'I don't see why.'

'Let someone else worry about the garden, for one thing. And your dad is quite right in saying I need to take steps now to avoid paying inheritance tax.'

'*You* wouldn't be paying it! Dad would. It would come out of your estate.'

'But I don't want my money going to the government.' Margaret set her spoon down in the saucer and turned her attention to him. 'Daniel, what have you done with Mia? There was no need for you to rush here this evening. I hope you didn't feel you couldn't cancel?'

Actually, it hadn't occurred to him. His sole thought had been to apologise to Freya.

'She's in the car.' He brushed a hand across his face, reluctant to confess even that much. He'd got a fifteen-year-old daughter he didn't trust to leave at home even for half an hour. What did that say about him?

*His life was a mess.* Other parents seemed to be turning out well-balanced young people, whereas he was heading towards a fully-fledged delinquent. What did Freya make of that?

*Of him?* For reasons he couldn't fathom he was suddenly interested in that. There was something particularly astute about the expression in her eyes when she looked at him. It made him feel she was weighing everything he said. Making a judgement. Probably finding him wanting.

'Oh, Daniel, bring her in. It's too cold for

her to be sitting out there, even if she's got her . . . whatever that thing is they all seem to be plugged into.'

Opposite, Freya smiled, her blue eyes holding a sudden sparkle. 'I suspect you mean an MP3 player.'

'Something like that,' Margaret agreed. 'Freya, be a darling and go and get her a glass of diet cola. She must be so fed up, sitting out there.'

'She's —'

'She's going to be frozen, Daniel. Just bring her in.'

Freya smiled and pushed her chair away from the table. She'd heard that tone in her grandmother's voice many times before, and it really did brook no argument. Even her dad had done as he was told when faced with that voice.

It was a shame she hadn't used it more often. If she'd been able to stay longer than that one summer holiday perhaps she'd have made different choices. Passed some exams.

For the umpteenth time that day she wondered what was motivating Mia. Her relationship with her dad was clearly fractured, but that didn't necessarily mean it was all his fault.

*A nice man doing his best.'* That was what her grandmother had said when she'd recounted the incident earlier.

And she honestly hadn't expected him to apologise. At least not in any sincere way. That changed things. Maybe she really had stumbled on a man with integrity?

She found a two-litre bottle of diet cola on the floor of the larder and poured some into a tall glass, carrying it back to the dining room. 'I found it.'

'Good. We can't leave Mia sitting out there. She'll be texting someone she shouldn't.'

'A little like me, then,' Freya said, setting it down on the tray.

'Except there wasn't texting when you were her age. You made your trouble in other ways.'

She'd certainly done that. But she'd had her reasons. When a person deliberately set out to push the self-destruct button there usually were reasons for it. *So what were Mia's?*

Freya turned her head as she heard father and daughter returning, taking in his bleak expression and her sulky one.

'Come and have a drink,' Margaret said as soon as they appeared.

Dry, Mia really was a very attractive girl. Her hair, which had looked a dirty honey shade earlier, was a dramatic strawberry blonde colour. She'd have been quite stunning if she'd smiled.

In case they didn't already know she was here under sufferance, Mia scarcely acknowledged that Margaret had spoken to her. Daniel ripped an exasperated hand through his hair and frowned at his daughter.

From this side of the fence it was almost comical to watch. Almost. It would never be quite that, because Freya knew what it felt like to carry a hard knot of anger inside. To feel lonely and frightened and so angry you didn't know what to do with yourself.

'Have you finished your tea?' Margaret asked.

Freya looked down at her empty cup. 'Yes.'

'Perhaps you'd take Daniel to look at the chiffonier and the table? I'll sit here and keep Mia company.'

'They're in the morning room,' Freya said, standing up.

Daniel quickly drained the last of his tea and set the cup back in the saucer. He glanced at his daughter. 'I won't be long.'

Mia hunched a shoulder and picked up her cola. This time Freya couldn't stop the tiny smile, then turned to look at Daniel and caught the quick flash of anger in his eyes. If Mia was looking to provoke a reaction from her father she'd succeeded.

A second glance at his daughter confirmed that she was completely aware of that. Whether or not Daniel was the root cause of Mia's anger, he was certainly the focus of it. 'If you want any more cola, I've left the bottle on the side in the kitchen.'

'Thank you.' Daniel spoke for her.

Freya turned her head and smiled. 'I assume you know where you're going?'

He nodded, and walked in the direction she'd pointed. Freya glanced back. With her dad out of the room Mia's whole belligerent air had vanished. She just looked sad. And quite a bit younger.

Margaret smiled at Freya across the top Mia's head. A look of complete understanding passed between them.

'Would you mind pouring me a second cup of tea, Mia?' Margaret asked. 'This hip of mine makes it difficult to get out of the chair.'

Freya followed Daniel out into the Minton-tiled hallway, with its stunning mahogany staircase sweeping upwards. She glanced across at him, wondering what had happened in their relationship to make it so strained. It might be arrogant, but she somehow felt that if she just had half an hour with Mia she might be able to help.

But it was none of her business. And Daniel was at least working on it. He lifted his hand to rub his temple, and Freya caught sight of his wedding ring.

*Where was Mia's mother in all this?* Her grandma hadn't mentioned her and she hadn't liked to ask. Just *'a nice man doing his best'.* That was all she'd said.

'Margaret's really good with her,' Daniel observed.

'With Mia?'

He nodded. 'This is one of the few places I can bring her.'

'Well, one way or another she's had practice.'

'You?'

Freya walked past him into the morning room. 'Don't tell me you weren't thinking that. I imagine you've heard at least five versions of my youthful misdemeanours.'

'One or two.'

It shouldn't hurt to hear what she already knew. But it did. Nevertheless, she liked him better for not lying to her. 'That's the trouble with Fellingham,' she said breezily. 'Nothing ever happens here, so they have to re-hash old stories. You'd think they might have found something else to talk about after this much time.'

'Your arrival re-sparked interest.'

'I just bet. Let me know if I'm under suspicion for murder. Or whether it's just abduction of minors —'

'I've apologised for that!'

Freya brushed an irritated hand across her face. 'True. My turn to apologise.'

'You can't have been much older than Mia when you left here.'

She took her hand away and caught the full force of his expression. Daniel really had the most incredible eyes. They seemed to offer a warmth and an acceptance she hadn't seen in the longest time.

'How old were you when you left?'

'Seventeen.'

Daniel nodded. 'Mia's fifteen. Not so very different in age, then.'

'Two years is a long time when you're a teenager,' Freya said quickly, wanting to make it absolutely clear that she didn't think Mia's life was on the same trajectory as hers had been. 'Fifteen to seventeen weren't good years for me, and I didn't make it easy for anyone to like me.'

Funny how you could encapsulate so much angst into a simple sentence. Thinking back now, she could see how she'd managed to antagonise pretty much everyone.

The consequence was that they weren't pleased to see her back. Everywhere she went she felt the whispers, the looks, and the constant speculation about what she wanted in coming back.

'Margaret's really glad you're here,' he said, as though he was able to read her mind.

She looked up at him and found he was watching her. For some inexplicable reason she wanted to cry. She bit on the side of her mouth in an effort to control the prickle of tears behind her eyes.

*How did he know what she'd been thinking?* If she wasn't careful she'd be pouring out every secret she'd ever had. Maybe she didn't have to. Maybe those dark brown eyes could see into her soul and read them all for himself?

'Half your trouble is because of that. Margaret was so excited when she knew you were coming that she mentioned it to one or two people . . .' He let his words taper off.

Freya's breath caught on an unexpected laugh. 'Yes, I know.' She hadn't quite believed she'd arrive until she'd actually stood on the doorstep.

'And you need to remember you're not seventeen any more,' he said, his voice soothing like velvet.

*No, she wasn't.* Right now she didn't feel

seventeen at all. Whatever it was Daniel Ramsay had, he should bottle it. It would make him a fortune. Even a cynic like her was dissolving at his feet in a pool of hormones.

*God help his poor wife.* Daniel would have more opportunity than most to stray. Maybe he did. Maybe that went some way to explaining Mia's anger?

Only that couldn't be right.

His hand moved to touch the chiffonier. 'Margaret wants to sell this?'

Freya nodded.

'Honestly, she'd do better to hang on to it for a few years. Dark wood isn't as popular as it was a few years back. It's all fashion. It'll have its time again.'

Daniel couldn't be that kind of man. If he was, her grandma would hardly describe him as 'doing his best'. And he was still wearing his wedding ring.

Freya pulled her eyes away from the unexpectedly sensual movement of his fingers running along the wood grain. 'It won't fit where she wants to go, so she doesn't have much of a choice.'

He pulled a face. 'I can't see sheltered housing suiting her.'

'Neither can I. But now they're building some in the village she's become quite keen . . . and I suppose it makes sense long-term. I don't mind, if it's what she really wants.'

He nodded and turned back to the chiffonier. 'This isn't going to make much more than five hundred. It's early nineteenth century, not particularly unusual, and big. Most houses just can't take a piece of furniture like this.'

'And it's ugly.' Freya moved away to stand nearer the door. She felt better with more space between them. One thing she'd learnt was that danger was best avoided. And, with a finely tuned instinct for survival, she knew Daniel Ramsay was dangerous.

'The barleytwist side columns are nice, but that's really all it's got going for it. I'd put a reserve of about four hundred on it but, I don't think it'll go much higher than that.'

'Anywhere?'

His eyes narrowed infinitesimally. 'If I thought she would get more elsewhere I'd tell her. Margaret's a friend, and my auction house isn't particularly looking for things to sell. With all the antiques programmes on TV recently, business is booming.'

'I didn't mean —'

'Yes, you did.' Daniel cut her off, and his

eyes held hers. He didn't even blink.

There was a beat of silence. *He really was a mind-reader.* 'Actually — yes, I probably did.'

Daniel thrust his hands deep into his jeans pockets. 'Is there any particular reason you think I'd do something underhand? Was it something I said or just a chemical reaction?'

'I don't know anything about you,' she said quickly.

'But you don't like me?'

Freya moved across to the dining table, pushed up into the corner of the room, and started to lift down the boxes stacked on it. 'I don't have to like you. I just need to be certain my grandmother isn't being taken for a ride.'

'And you think I'd do that?'

'I think your business needs a good injection of capital, and I think you want quality pieces passing through your auction house even if the owners would get a better price elsewhere.'

The silence was longer this time. 'You don't take any prisoners, do you?'

She shrugged. 'What's the point? The sooner we get finished here, the sooner you can take Mia home. What do you think of this?'

Daniel moved back to look at the bulbous legs of the table. 'Do you have the extra leaves?'

She nodded, feeling unexpectedly mean. 'Three. Behind the door over there.'

'What does it measure when fully extended?'

'Three hundred and ten centimetres.' Daniel crossed over to look at the other pieces of the table and she added, 'There's a scratch on one of the leaves. I can't remember which one now. I think the back one.'

He looked for a moment. 'It's quite deep, but that won't affect the value much. This will most likely go to a dealer who'll be able to sort that.' Daniel turned back to her. 'I'd no idea Margaret had this. It's lovely. Why doesn't she use it?'

'She did. When I was younger. We used to have big Sunday lunches.'

Daniel's eyes softened again, making her want to run away and hide. What did he imagine he was seeing when he looked at her? There was no way on earth he could know how much she'd loved those Sundays. Loved the huge knickerbocker glorys her grandma had made especially for her.

'She's not used it for years, so there's no point hanging on to it,' she said brusquely.

He nodded. 'It's worth something in the region of three thousand pounds. I'd certainly want to see a reserve of at least two thousand on it. Is there anything else you want me to look at while I'm here?'

'There's a clock in the hallway. She doesn't really want to sell that, but if she does end up in Cymbeline Court it'll never fit.' Freya led the way back into the hall and stood in front of it. 'I quite like this, actually.'

'It's lovely.'

Freya looked over her shoulder. 'Don't you need to look at it more closely?'

'It's a New Jersey Federal mahogany long-case clock, and it's a gem. I've looked at it before.' Daniel gave a wry smile. 'Every time I come here. Honesty compels me to admit this might be something you'd do well to sell elsewhere. We haven't had a clock of this quality in our saleroom for months. I'll look into it.'

'So how much is it worth?'

'Conservatively, about twenty thousand.'

'Why so much more than the table? There seem to be loads of clocks about.'

He walked forward and stroked his fingers down the side of the case, as though he were touching something precious. 'This one is attributable to a known cabinet maker. William Dawes worked in Elizabethtown into the first decade of the 1800s. This clock was probably made at the turn of the century.'

'So it's American? How the heck do you know that?'

Daniel smiled. 'Look.' He pointed up at the clock face. 'In a European clock you'd expect to see a brass dial, but metal was hard to come by in America so they used iron and painted it white.'

'Ah. So, how do you know it's by this William Dawes?'

'It's got "William Dawes, Hackensack" on the face. That's a good clue.'

He was laughing at her. Again. A sexy glint lighting his dark brown eyes. It made her feel flustered.

*What was the matter with her today?* Her whole survival plan was based around control. Control was everything.

But there was something about his brown eyes which ripped through her defences. Made her wish . . .

*Damn it!*

She turned away. He was *married.* And she wasn't interested in a man who was prepared to lie to someone they'd promised to love.

'Are you done?' Margaret called from the dining room.

'Are we?'

Freya turned back to him. 'Everything else is small. I can bring them to you when we're more organised. The bigger things we're going to need to have collected.'

He nodded. 'That's a flat fee, and we'll take it out of the profits after the sale. Just let me know what you want to do.'

'It's not my decision.'

His smile was slow in coming, but all the more sexy for that. Her stomach flipped over in a way she couldn't control. 'Somehow I doubt that,' he said, walking past her. 'All finished. I'll put my valuations in writing, and pop them through your door in the next couple of days.'

'Lovely.'

Freya hovered in the doorway, much as he had done earlier. He was wrong. If it *were* her decision her grandma would sell absolutely nothing and leave her entire estate to her favourite charity.

But her grandma was determined to sell. And she would probably give her son a large chunk of the profits, because she still couldn't bring herself to say no to him. And she'd use Daniel's auction house, whatever anyone said, because she liked him.

Freya looked over at Mia, who had finished her drink and was already standing up. It couldn't be much fun for her, being dragged round to valuations. But that could only be because Daniel didn't trust her to stay at home.

Did Mum work late, then? She was rabidly curious to know what kind of woman Daniel was married to. Someone small and fluffy, she reckoned. Or, she thought, looking at Mia, some elegant redhead who saved lives.

'We'd better go. Don't get up,' he said to Margaret, who predictably ignored him.

Freya stood back to let them pass. She caught Mia's eye and winked.

Mia smiled. 'Thanks for the cola.'

'Any time.'

Daniel placed a hand on his daughter's shoulders and steered her towards the door.

'Bye,' Margaret said with a wave, shutting the door behind them as Daniel's car drove away. 'Did you like him any better?'

The speculative gleam in her grandmother's eyes had Freya walking briskly back through to the dining room. 'He knows more about antiques than I thought he would, which is a start,' she said casually, stacking the cups on the tray. 'Though I still think you'd do better finding a larger auction house.'

'I told you earlier — I'd rather do business with someone I like.'

'Most people at least settle for competence in their chosen profession.' Freya shuffled the saucers to one side to make space for the teapot. 'I don't think I've ever seen an office like his.'

'I doubt it's like that all the time. He's making do with temporary help at the moment, and that's never going to be as good as a permanent person, is it?'

Freya snorted. 'I'm surprised he's ever had a permanent person. His office is like a sorting office, and every bit as dirty. If you spent much time in there you'd have to be fumigated when you came out.'

'Then, of course, there's Mia,' Margaret offered, as she watched her granddaughter with intense amusement. 'She must take up a lot of his time.'

Freya smiled. 'Which is a dig at me, I suppose?' she said, picking up the tray.

'I can't honestly say my son ever put off anything because of your antics. Daniel's a very different kind of father.'

'I like Mia.'

'So do I. She's a bright thing, but unless she's careful she'll waste it.'

Freya stopped at the doorway. 'I didn't.'

'You were unusually driven. I don't think Mia's the same,' Margaret said, following behind her. 'Unless I've missed my mark, I reckon that girl is floundering. It's no time for a girl to be without her mother.'

'Is she?' Any number of possible scenarios waltzed through Freya's head. Perhaps she'd had an affair and left Mia behind? But then *why* would Daniel still be wearing his ring?

Margaret cut through her thoughts. 'You remember Anna Jameson, as was?'

'Yes. I think. Vaguely. Sophia Jameson's elder sister — ?' Freya stopped. 'You're telling me Mia Ramsay is *Anna Jameson's* daughter? I don't believe it!'

Her memories of Anna were sketchy. She was a few years older but — she frowned — from what she recalled Anna had been long, thin, and very, very good.

*How in heck had Anna managed to attract a man as sexy as Daniel Ramsay?*

'Anna died . . .' Margaret hesitated, pulling the necessary information together in her head. 'Oh, it must be three years ago last October. Not so very long before Christmas anyway.'

*Died.* 'Anna's dead?'

Her grandmother nodded. 'Horribly young. She was only in her early thirties, as I remember. I could work it out exactly if I sat down and thought about it.'

71

'That's awful. I — I hadn't heard that.'

'There's no reason why you should have,' Margaret replied, clutching at the doorjamb, her face convulsing in a sudden sharp pain. 'It's not as though you kept up with Sophia. You didn't like her much, did you?'

She hadn't liked either of them, if she were honest. Sophia had been a real thorn in the flesh. One of those catty girls who seemed to fool everyone into believing they were all sweetness and light.

Anna had been the middle-class embodiment of perfection. Freya hadn't really known her — just about her. Anna had been the best cellist in the school. She'd been a straight 'A' grade student. She'd had the kind of hair that stayed beautifully plaited all day. Red hair.

*Hair exactly the colour of Mia's.* Hell, but she was stupid. Freya frowned as a new thought popped into her head. 'Anna can't have been very old when she had Mia, can she?'

Margaret's mouth twisted into a wry smile. 'No.'

'So, how old was she?'

'All I know — and it's not much — is that Anna had to drop out of university when she found out she was pregnant. Andrew and Lorna were mortified, of course.'

'Couldn't she have carried on at uni? Gone back after the birth or something?'

'I don't know. You don't imagine anyone ever speaks about it, do you?' her grandmother said in mock horror. 'We all go about pretending we can't do our maths.'

That fitted snugly with everything she'd ever known about the Jamesons. *But Daniel?* That wasn't such an easy fit.

Why would he have got involved with someone like Anna Jameson? Had he loved her? Or just been trapped by circumstances?

He was still wearing her ring three years after her death. He must have loved her. Must still love her.

Freya stepped down in the kitchen and set the tray down on the side. But any man who'd think about getting involved with any member of the Jameson family needed his head examined. And to move here, to be near them . . .

'Why the frown?' Margaret asked, coming in behind her.

'If Mia's fifteen, I was still here when she was born. How come I didn't know anything about it?'

'Anna didn't come back here. I think she went to stay with some friends of her mother's sister.'

'Until after the baby was born?'

'I really don't know the details, Freya. The official line was that Anna was married, had had a baby and was living very happily in London. The next thing we heard was that Anna had been diagnosed with cancer. Presumably she wanted to be near her family, because they moved back here about six or seven months after that. All very difficult for Daniel, I imagine, as they're not the easiest of families. And Anna was dead inside of a year.'

# Chapter Four

Freya knew Mrs Runton had been talking about her the minute she walked into the trendy farm shop. She knew it from the sudden awkward hiatus in the conversation, and the way neither she nor the girl at the till would meet her eyes.

She took in a deep breath and made a show of looking at the jars of jams and chutneys, refusing to follow her instinct and walk back out.

'How's Margaret?' Mrs Runton asked. 'I've been meaning to call.'

Freya looked up. It was weird to think the nosy old biddy must be possessed of a first name. But if she was she'd never heard it. Mrs Runton, in her cheap anorak and sensible boots, had always been a disapproving figure.

'She's well, thank you.'

'And your mother?'

Freya turned back to the rows of preserves

and selected a champagne and strawberry jam.

'I haven't liked to ask Margaret since the divorce,' Mrs Runton continued. 'I don't suppose they're on particularly good terms now.'

With calm deliberation Freya selected two different chutneys. 'She's well. Just finished renovating her first two *gîtes*.'

'Already!' she exclaimed, as though she'd already known all about the château in Normandy and her mother's plans.

Freya found herself smiling. For the first time since she'd arrived in Fellingham she found it all slightly ridiculous, rather than painful.

'And your father's remarried . . . ?'

*Not only had he remarried, he'd done it eight years ago — which only went to show how truly meaningless this conversation was.*

'Very happily, yes.' To the perfect trophy wife, if she really wanted to know.

Freya's head whipped round at the sound of the shop bell.

'Freya!'

Daniel looked almost as shocked to see her as she was him. Though, when she took a second to think about it, it wasn't so very surprising. They'd been bound to run into each other again eventually. Only she didn't feel quite ready to yet. She hadn't even begun to process the information that he was Anna Jameson's widower. *That he was single.*

'I didn't spot your car.'

'I hope it's still there.'

'You should be all right. Fellingham's car crime figures are fairly low.' He smiled, but it looked like hard work somehow. In fact, he looked tired. Not surprising, since he'd gone home with a very angry teenager.

'I'm here to pick up a quick lunch.'

'I've been sent to get "essentials",' she said, holding out her basket.

Mrs Runton leant between them to pick up a jar of marmalade. 'Your father settled in Beadnell, didn't he, Freya? I'm sure I heard that.'

'That's right.'

'I was saying to Mary Davidson just yesterday . . .'

Freya settled some elderflower cordial into her basket and added a box of six fresh eggs, letting Mrs Runton's voice hum away in the background.

'. . . we haven't had a doctor in the village like him since he left. He was a wonderful man.'

Daniel moved across to the chiller section, and Freya's eyes followed him. She'd have loved to know what kind of evening he'd had with Mia — but she couldn't really ask. She'd also have liked to ask whether he was still actively mourning Mia's mother. And whether that was why he was still wearing her ring.

*Anna Jameson.* He'd been married to Anna Jameson.

That was just so difficult to accept. In fact, the concept of Anna Jameson being overwhelmed by any kind of sexual activity to the extent that she forgot to use contraception was unbelievable.

'You remember Muriel, I assume?' Mrs Runton continued inexorably. 'Her daughter Jenny was in your year at school. The same year as Anna's younger sister,' she said, pulling Daniel into the conversation. 'Sophia was in Jenny's year, wasn't she?'

'I don't think I know, Pamela,' he answered, a cheese and pickle sandwich in hand. 'Anna never mentioned her.'

*Pamela* Runton, Freya registered with a sense of satisfaction. It was nice to have a mystery solved — though Mrs suited her better. Pamela seemed too human.

'You've met our Daniel already, then, Freya?' Her small dark eyes looked curiously from one to the other.

Freya risked a fleeting glance in his direction, wondering how he liked being tarred by association.

'Yesterday.'

'Oh?' the elderly woman said, pausing hopefully, in case either one of them would voluntarily add any more. 'Sophia didn't mention that earlier. And I saw her not half an hour ago . . .'

Something snapped inside Freya. Her new-found sense of freedom evaporated as quickly as it had come. *They'd been talking about her.* Mrs Runton and Sophia *bloody* Jameson. If she *was* still a Jameson. Of *course* they had. It was all anyone in this closed-off, narrow-minded village had to do.

Freya fought against the sudden spurt of anger. Sophia probably still managed to spread poison with that butter-wouldn't-melt kind of smile on her face. Still managed to stick the knife in with supercilious graciousness and that kind of 'who me?' expression if anyone ever challenged her on it.

She just wanted to scream at the claustrophobia of it all.

'If you've finished your shopping, Freya,' Daniel said, coming to stand beside her, 'perhaps we could grab a coffee and discuss which sale Margaret wants to put her furniture in? I've got twenty minutes or so before I need to be back at the saleroom.'

*He was rescuing her.* Rescuing himself, too, maybe. Freya looked up and caught the expression in his eyes, which clearly said he didn't want to be left to the mercy of Mrs Runton, either.

'I know Margaret wants it all settled as quickly as possible . . .'

Freya set her basket on the low shelf at the till point. 'I've got a few minutes.'

The girl behind the till slowly scanned each item.

Mrs Runton came to stand beside her. 'Oh, is Margaret going to sell up?'

'She's thinking about it.' Freya placed her credit card in the machine. 'Nothing's absolutely decided yet.'

'I suppose that's why you're here . . . ?'

Freya ignored the hopeful way she left the question hanging.

'Tell Margaret I'll be round next Monday with the flowers from church, to hear all about her plans.'

Freya almost managed a smile. Her mouth tilted, even if there was no softness in her eyes. 'I'll pack these away in the car,' she said, looking over at Daniel. 'And meet you outside in a few minutes.'

'Great.'

She gathered up the last of her things. Inside her head she was screaming. Living in this village was like living in a goldfish bowl.

Freya pushed open the door and escaped into the chill of the January morning. She took in a couple of huge gulps of air before walking towards her car. She hated this place. Everyone was going round and round, doing the same things they'd always done, watching and sniping at everyone else.

She tucked her bags into the footwell of the passenger seat and slammed the door shut. How could her grandmother bear to be a part of it? Everyone sniffing about in her business. Everyone thinking they knew exactly what was going on behind closed doors when they most certainly did not.

'Are you all right?' Daniel said, coming up quietly behind her. His hand reached out, and then fell back by his side without touching her.

Freya twisted a stray lock of hair behind her ear. 'Just angry. I can't even pick up bread and milk without running into someone who thinks —'

She broke off abruptly and pulled a hand across her eyes. 'I'm sorry.'

'What?'

'I don't mean to let it get to me. Sorry. It

doesn't matter.'

He didn't believe her. One glance at his face told her that, but he let it go.

'Look, do you want that coffee or not?'

*Did she? She wasn't sure what she wanted.* He wasn't married, but he was a potential complication she just didn't need right now. A year out, a year free of men, was what she'd promised herself.

'Or would you rather make your escape while Pamela is still marvelling that she knows someone who's renovated a couple of *gîtes?*'

She looked up into his dark eyes, wickedly laughing, and felt much of her anger evaporate. 'Is that what she's doing?'

'Oh, yes. Though she's not at all surprised because "Christine always did like her foreign holidays",' he said, in a passable imitation of Mrs Runton.

Freya's chuckle caught at the back of her throat. She pulled up the collar of her jacket, saying, 'She's a horrid woman.'

'Not so much. Just a bored one.' He placed his hands deep in his pockets. 'Come and have a coffee. Take some deep breaths and forget all about her.'

It was tempting — but probably not wise *because* it was so tempting.

Not wise at all. Then a new thought

popped into her head. Unless his sister-in-law's character had changed beyond recognition, Daniel couldn't have heard a single good thing about her — so why was he bothering? He must *really* want to sell her grandma's things.

'Are you sure your reputation will survive being seen in public with the scarlet woman of Fellingham?'

'It might even go up a notch.' His smile twisted. 'You might not like what people are saying about you, but I'm more than a little weary of my own reputation,' Daniel said, bringing his hands out of his pockets. 'Go on — tell me I've not been described to you as a "good boy" or words to that effect.'

'Apparently, you're *nice.*'

'Nice?' Daniel hung his head.

'Uh-huh.'

'Not exciting, is it?' he said, and she began to laugh. Maybe those glinting eyes were more of an indicator of his character than his choice of wife.

'Come on — have a coffee. I owe you anyway, for having been so unreasonable yesterday. Let's call this a peace offering.'

'I didn't behave particularly well myself.'

He shrugged. 'If you think I've been manipulating Margaret then it's understandable. I like you better for looking out for her. She's kind of special.'

'Yes, she is.' Freya looked up into those dark eyes and made a snap decision. *It was just coffee.* And they did have business to discuss. Of a sort. 'Where do we go to get this drink?'

'Annabelle's.' He pointed back towards the courtyard. 'Best teacakes in the business.'

'Great.'

They started across the courtyard and Daniel glanced across at her. 'You know, I've got no hidden agenda as regards Margaret. I just like her. You always know exactly where you are with her. And she's got a good heart.'

'She's equally complimentary about you.'

He smiled. 'You still don't like it, though, do you? A natural sceptic.'

*Life had made her like that.* It didn't sound so wonderful, though. Scepticism wasn't a character trait people generally aspired to.

'I'm not sure what I think.' Freya glanced up at him. Truth be told, she wanted to believe him. Tall, dark, clever, handsome. Surely there had to be a catch somewhere? 'You drop round for cups of tea, change her fuses, dispose of wandering rodents . . .'

The glint in his brown eyes intensified. 'Guilty.'

'Why would you do that?'

'She's a friend.'

She shrugged. That was the bit she had trouble accepting. 'I suppose I don't believe anyone does anything without some kind of agenda.'

'But then I'm *nice*,' he shot back quickly.

Freya felt a smile start in her chest and work out from there.

*God, he was good.*

She looked over her shoulder. 'I'm reserving judgement on that one.'

His laugh was a bark. Sexy. Staggeringly sexy. What would his reaction be if she told him she'd just sold her business for two and a half million? Would he be intimidated by it? Unable to look at her without seeing figures stamped across her forehead?

She weaved her way through the oak tables and settled herself at one with a clear view of the courtyard. 'What are these?' she asked, turning in her seat to look at the oak chairs with a shelf at the back. 'Are they from a church?'

'Annabelle bought a job lot at the auction. St Andrew's Church over in Kilbury ripped out all its pews eighteen months ago and turned itself into a community centre. We sold everything. Even the pulpit.'

Freya spun back and picked up the menu.

'That's a shame.'

'Why? I'd have guessed you were all for progress.'

'Some things should stay the same.' Like her grandma's house, she realised with a pang.

How unreasonable, considering she'd not visited in more than a decade. But it was comforting to know it was all going on the same. That there was still a walnut tree in the centre of what would otherwise have been a perfect croquet lawn. Still a blue patchwork quilt on the bed in the guest room. Still a small blue dish on the kitchen windowsill, where her grandmother put her rings when she was washing up.

'I'm all for that,' he said, smiling across at her.

'Have St Mark's done the same?'

Daniel shook his head. 'Nothing's changed there. The pews are still being lovingly polished every Friday night, and there's a team of flower arrangers who descend the following Saturday.'

'Good.' Freya smiled and looked down at the menu. 'I used to love St Mark's.'

'You did?'

She understood his surprise — but then, like pretty much everyone else, he didn't know just how many arguments there had been at home. The old vicar had got used to her coming over, and he'd let her sit and read quietly. One of the few who hadn't been blinded by her parents' sham of a marriage.

'Wouldn't that shock Mrs Runton?' Freya said flippantly, turning as the door chimed. An elderly couple struggled to manage the step and lift their shopping basket in. Daniel was on his feet in a moment.

'Thanks, Dan.' The man smiled and nodded across at her.

'I'm sorry I didn't make it out to the farm yesterday.'

'Don't give that a thought. I'm just glad you found your girl before she got herself into any trouble.'

'I'll give you a call later on today and we can reschedule.'

'Righto.' The elderly man nodded. 'There's no mad hurry.'

Freya moved her chair out of the way to make it easier for the couple to manoeuvre the shopping trolley further into the tearoom. She scooted it back in when they'd passed. 'Did you miss many appointments yesterday?'

'One or two.' Daniel sat down and rubbed a hand across the back of his neck. 'It was a long and very difficult day.' He looked up.

'Incidentally, why did you lie about that cigarette?'

'I didn't.' He raised one eyebrow and she smiled. 'Not exactly. I very carefully asked if you had a problem with it being mine.'

'Yes, I got that. But why?'

'Honestly?'

Daniel nodded.

Freya slipped her sheepskin jacket off her shoulders and let it fall on the back of her chair. 'Mia looked at me for help. And,' she said watching for his reaction, 'I thought she was dead meat already.'

The muscle in the side of his cheek twitched. 'True enough, I suppose.'

'I like her.'

He looked up, seemingly surprised. 'I like her, too. But some of the things she's doing at the moment . . .' He pulled the wooden table number towards him and rotated it between his long fingers. 'I hate her smoking. She must think I'm an idiot if she thinks I can't smell it on her breath.'

'I don't suppose she thinks that.' Freya looked out of the window, distracted by a glimpse of Mrs Runton's red anorak. 'I suspect she wants you to know. On some level. She's just pushing against the boundaries. Working out where they are.'

'It certainly feels that way.' Daniel sat up

straighter and smiled. 'So, what are we having?'

'I think I'd like a filter coffee to go with my toasted teacake.'

'Sounds good.' The merest nod in the direction of the waitress brought her over. 'Filter coffee and toasted teacake, twice. Thank you.' He waited until she'd written down their order and then asked, 'How's Annabelle feeling?'

'I think she'll be back tomorrow.'

'What's the matter with Annabelle?' Freya asked, as the waitress disappeared behind a half-door.

'Flu. It decimated most of Fellingham over Christmas. Margaret had it, too. Did she tell you?'

Freya turned back. 'Yes.'

'Is that why you're here?'

'Partly.'

'And partly not?' His lips twitched as she said nothing. 'But you don't intend to tell me?'

'I haven't decided if you're nice yet. I like to make my own judgements.'

His eyes glinted. 'Fair enough.'

The waitress returned with the two coffees and a small jug of cream. Brown sugar crystals sat in a small bowl in the centre of the table.

It was quaint. A real touch of Ye Olde England. If the waitress had been wearing a starched white apron over a long black dress she wouldn't have looked out of place. Freya let her eyes wander up to the exposed beams and felt herself relax. This was lovely.

She looked back and caught Daniel watching her. Something about his expression made her feel as though heat was rushing up from her toes. His thumb moved against his gold wedding band, twisting it round.

She ought to be careful. Daniel might be officially single, but he still chose to wear his wedding band. Men who were looking for a new relationship didn't do that.

Which was probably just as well. She wasn't looking, either.

Freya smiled and forced her mind to think of something else. 'You know, when I left Fellingham the farm shop was basically a lock-up and the barns were just that. This whole Craft Village idea is amazing.'

'It's better in summer, when there are tables out across the courtyard. Some weekends there's a string quartet playing. A couple of times I've heard a jazz band here.'

Freya looked out of the window and imagined the hanging baskets full of lobelia and busy Lizzies.

'Though Christmas is kind of magical,

with all the lights. And over there,' he said, pointing to a corner near the bead shop, 'is home to Santa's Grotto.'

'Santa's Grotto?' she repeated.

'In aid of the local hospice. It's been there every year for the past three years.'

'And who gets to be Father Christmas?'

The waitress returned for a second time with their teacakes, and butter freshly curled into two round dishes. Having spent most of the last few years religiously counting every calorie, Freya made the decision to simply indulge. The butter oozed across the top of the teacake and dripped down onto her plate.

'We have a rota.'

Freya looked up. 'For . . . ?'

'Father Christmas.'

'Oh.' And then, as she caught up with the conversation, 'You're telling me *you've* been Father Christmas?'

'Obviously not *the* Father Christmas. He's too busy to come. But I think I'm quite good at it.'

'Being nice?' He wasn't just *nice,* he was chocolate coated. His eyes glinted, and the effect was rather like balsamic vinegar cutting through a sweet dish. Not too nice. Daniel had hidden depths. And when they were combined with the niceness the effect was lethal.

'Exactly. Though I'm never quite sure why parents bring their children to sit on the knee of a complete stranger.'

Laughter hovered at the edge of her mouth. 'Is there much knee-sitting involved these days?'

'Not so much.'

'There you go, then.' She took a bite of her teacake. 'I've not had one of these in years.'

'Why?'

'I haven't had time to sit in coffee shops. Far too busy.'

Daniel lifted the cream jug and let it hover above her cup.

'Please.'

He swirled in the cream, and then poured some on top of his own coffee. 'And too busy to come to Fellingham?'

She looked up, searching for some kind of criticism in his question — but there was none. Only interest.

'That's what Margaret told me when I asked about her family once.'

'I've been abroad a lot.' Freya knew she was trying to justify what was really unjustifiable.

Of course it would have been possible to come to Fellingham before. It was a mere fifty minutes down the motorway from London. The truth was she hadn't wanted to. They'd spoken on the telephone. Met at her dad's. Her grandma had also come up to London — though that hadn't happened for a good two years.

'And now?'

And now that didn't seem like such a good excuse. Her grandma's hip was significantly worse than she'd ever let on, and her dad was becoming more and more persistent in his efforts to get a chunk of his inheritance early.

Freya's fingers played on the handle of her coffee cup. 'Now I'm between jobs. I'm taking a year out to travel.'

'Anywhere in particular?'

'I'd like to spend some time in Australia. I've got friends who've just returned to Melbourne from London. I'd like to see them.'

'Melbourne's great.' He lifted his cup and sipped. 'Anna and I spent some time there in . . .' He frowned. 'I can't remember. Years ago. We went during the summer break of Anna's first year at uni.' There was a small beat of silence before he added, 'Brunswick Street. You ought to go there. It's . . . fun.'

*Fun.* She couldn't imagine Anna Jameson ever having fun. But Daniel had chosen to marry her. *And he still wore her ring — even*

*though she was dead.* That part really fascinated her. Half the 'happily' married men
she knew slipped their rings off on a fairly
regular basis.

Perhaps that was just the men she knew.
Daniel appeared to still want to wear a
symbol that tied him to his late wife.

'I only heard yesterday that your wife had
died. I'm so sorry.'

'You didn't know before?'

She shook her head.

'I'm surprised.' Daniel lifted the spoon in
the sugar bowl and twisted it about, then
carefully patted the sides so that it made a
kind of desert dune scene. 'It's usually the
first thing anyone says about me.'

'Well, my only source is my grandma —
and she's not really one for gossip.'

'No, she isn't.' He smiled and sat back in
his chair. 'She hasn't told me a great deal
about you, either.'

'So you only know what you've heard in
the village?'

'That's about it.' He smiled again. 'And I
only believe about half of it.'

Freya laughed and looked down at her
teacake. She loved the way he smiled. The
lines at the corner of his eyes. Why did
crow's feet look so darn sexy on men?

'You wouldn't tell me yesterday, but how

long are you planning on staying in Fellingham?'

'I really don't know. This was going to be a flying visit.'

'But?' he prompted.

'But my grandma's hip is much worse than she told me. I suppose I'd like to see her have the operation before I disappear out of the country.'

'Which could be a while if she insists on waiting for the NHS.'

'I know,' Freya said, with a grimace.

'She'd love it if you stayed.' He hesitated. 'If you're between jobs, and want to stay in the village for a bit without eating into your reserves, you could always come and work for me.'

'Pardon?'

'Why not?' His fingers still played with the sugar spoon. 'You're out of work, and I'm in desperate need for some kind of administrative help.'

'You don't know anything about me.'

'I know you can string two words together, and you can answer the telephone. If it turns out you can type with more than two fingers you'll be an improvement on what I'm being sent.'

Freya laughed — mainly from shock. She couldn't quite believe she was being offered a job as a kind of Girl Friday — or that a significant part of her thought it might be fun to accept.

'What did you do before?'

'It was . . . computer based.'

That was true enough. She'd infinitely prefer it if people in Fellingham remained unaware that she'd built up a successful dot com business, selling natural beauty products worldwide.

'Can you do websites?'

'Actually, I can.' In fact, that was how it had all begun.

'In that case,' Daniel said, sitting back in his chair, 'I'm begging.'

Freya hid her smile behind her coffee cup. 'But I don't want to work for you.'

'Is that a straight no?'

'Pretty much.'

He laughed. 'It was worth a try. Who knows? Perhaps the next person I get might be the answer to my prayers.'

Freya looked at him curiously. 'Can't you contact a different agency if you're not happy with the service the one you're using is giving you?'

He shook his head. 'There are only two agencies in this neck of the woods, and both say there's a dearth of good temps at the moment. Last year there was a glut. But not this year.'

'The good ones will be going somewhere else,' Freya remarked, finishing her teacake. 'Be a bit demanding —'

'You would?'

'I would! If it were my business.'

His eyes were laughing again. She wasn't sure how he managed to do that. His face was completely passive, but his eyes were . . . dancing. She felt herself melting from the inside out. She was such a sucker for men with eyes like that. It was definitely her Achilles' heel.

'Temporary staff are expensive —'

'Don't I know it.'

'— and I like to get value for money,' she said, picking up her cup.

'Maybe I should just get *you* to phone the agency? See if you can get them to magic up someone who's actually employable.'

'I bet I could. I'm a good manager of people, I think.'

'You *think?*'

'Well, it's not rocket science.'

His eyes were sparkling with laughter. *So sexy.*

'I just state what I want very clearly, and then I make sure it gets done.'

'Doesn't work if the person you're speaking to isn't capable of doing the job.'

97

'I suppose not,' Freya agreed, looking at him curiously. But then she hadn't ever employed anyone who wasn't.

She'd never employed anyone on a whim, either. And she wouldn't have had a window painted shut in her office. And she most certainly would have been difficult enough to make any agency think twice about putting her to the bottom of their 'to keep happy' list.

*But then she wasn't nice.*

Freya picked up her handbag. 'I really should get back. Did you want me to say anything to my grandma about different sales, or was that a ruse?'

'Definitely a ruse. There's no question Margaret's items should go into our monthly Antiques and Collectables sale.'

'As opposed to . . . ?'

'The weekly general sale,' he said, with a glance across at the waitress, who came over with the bill on a china saucer. Daniel took his wallet out of the inside pocket of his jacket and placed down a crisp twenty-pound note.

For the first time in a very long time Freya wasn't sure what she should do. She might know a lot about how to run a business, but she was out of her depth when it came to the simple social things. It was the part of her life she'd neglected. 'How much do I owe you?'

'My treat.'

'I —'

'You can pay next time.' The expression in his eyes let loose a million butterflies in her stomach.

No doubt he didn't mean that the way it sounded.

*But what if he did?*

She fingered her earring self-consciously. 'Thank you.'

The waitress came back with the change. Daniel slid his wallet back into his pocket. 'I'll contact Margaret to arrange a sensible time to collect her furniture, but it won't be until after this month's sale.'

'When is that?' Freya asked, standing up.

'Friday week. The Antiques and Collectables sale is held on the last Friday of every month. I'll drop you round the catalogue for the one up-and-coming, and then you'll probably feel happier about the whole thing.'

'I just want to know she's getting the best possible price. That house is her life's work.'

His eyes smiled. She swore they did. A slow lilting smile that began at the centre and worked out. The butterflies in her stomach changed to something which felt more akin to a million and one ants marching around in concentric circles.

'I know. That wasn't a criticism. I'll drop round the valuations as soon as I possibly can — only I'm without office help at the moment.'

She laughed, picking up her jacket. 'Get on to that agency again. Thanks for the coffee.'

'Any time.'

Daniel watched as she ran across the courtyard, the edges of her short skirt flipping round her thighs.

*She really did have longest of long legs.* And the sexiest purple high-heeled boots he thought he'd ever seen.

He pulled a hand across his face and let out a breath in one steady stream. Considering everything, it would be better if he didn't focus too much on Freya Anthony's unquestionable sex appeal. He'd got a daughter to parent, and that was going to take every bit of his energy for the foreseeable future.

'Where did she get that jacket?'

Daniel turned his head to look at the waitress, suddenly conscious they'd both been standing looking out of the window. 'London, I imagine.'

'It must have cost the earth,' Hannah said,

placing a teapot on her tray. 'It's just like the ones you see in *Vogue* and that.'

*Was it?* Daniel's eyes wandered back to Freya, moments before she disappeared round the corner. Probably. It was a timely reminder. Freya Anthony was high maintenance. Too rich for his blood even if he had the time to pursue anything — which he hadn't.

Just as well she thought the idea of working for him — even temporarily — was a bad idea, because the temptation might just have been too much.

'Is it true she's going out with a rock star?'

Daniel pulled on his jacket. 'I've no idea.'

But privately he doubted it. There was such nonsense being talked about her. The rock star boyfriend was just one of many possible explanations floating around to account for her expensive car.

There'd been no mention of any boyfriend in her travel plans. Perhaps Sophy was closest, with her 'between relationships' theory. His eyes helplessly followed as her sleek car disappeared from view.

She seemed like someone who was at a bit of a loss for direction — and a complete contradiction. Confident and yet vulnerable.

He shook his head. He ought to be getting back to work, not speculating about the personality traits of a stunning blonde who would ultimately leave Fellingham as fast as her designer boots would take her.

'Thanks, Hannah. Say hi to Annabelle.' Daniel stepped out into the windy morning, shutting the door of the teashop behind him. He lifted the collar of his jacket against the rain.

He liked her. Simple as that. He hadn't expected to, but he did. With her, he felt like a person. Not Anna's poor husband. Mia's unfortunate father. Professor Jameson's bereaved son-in-law. Nor in any of the other pigeonholes people were all too ready to put him in.

And he liked the fact Freya didn't seem inclined to believe she ought to fill the space in his life created by Anna's death. That made a change.

Why did women so often feel that about widowers? It was almost as though you hit the eighteen-month mark and it flicked some kind of switch that sent out a subliminal message across a fifty-mile radius.

He wasn't ready for that. Still wasn't, after three years. True enough, the raw ache of the early days had gone — but he wasn't ready to put another woman into his life. Mia really did need to be the centre of his world.

The phone in his pocket beeped and he pulled it out of his pocket, barely needing to glance at the familiar number of Kilbury Comprehensive to know it was his daughter's school. The familiar sense of foreboding and sheer exhaustion spread through him. 'Ramsay.'

The voice at the other end belonged to one of the receptionists. He could even pinpoint which one. Carol. Grey bobbed hair. Extremely controlled. 'Mr Ramsay?'

'Yes.'

'The head has asked me to contact you to say there's been an incident this morning, involving Mia and another girl in her year. They're both safe, but he'd like you to come in to discuss what we do next.'

It took every ounce of control he had not to swear, long and loud. Even so, it wasn't entirely unexpected — considering the mood Mia had woken up in. She'd been ripe for trouble. Again. He closed his eyes against the images the word 'incident' conjured up. 'Do I need to come now?'

'Preferably some time this morning.'

Daniel glanced at his wristwatch. 'I've got an appointment in fifteen minutes, which should last half an hour or so. I'll come straight after that.'

'Thank you. I'll let Mr Oxendale know.'

He had to ask. 'What kind of incident?'

The well-modulated voice at the other end of the phone hesitated. 'Would you like to speak to Mr Oxendale now? I can see if he's available.'

Daniel could almost sense Carol's finger hovering over the call transfer button, and he rushed to answer. 'There's no need. I'll be in within the hour.'

He ended the call and slipped the phone back into his pocket. He could wait to speak to the head. For now it was enough to know Mia was physically safe. Whatever bad news was coming, he'd prefer to hear it with his daughter sitting in the same room and hearing every word. This was getting serious. If she'd reached the end of the road as far as Kilbury Comprehensive was concerned, what then?

# Chapter Five

Freya put the last of the china in the box. 'You're absolutely sure you want this to go in the general sale?'

Margaret looked up from her position, comfortably surrounded by old recipe books. 'Just get it out of the way. I've never particularly liked that set, and it'll be one less box to fall over.'

Freya stretched masking tape across the top and smoothed it out. 'If you're *absolutely* sure, I'll take it down with the other two.'

'Good.'

'I won't be long.'

'Be nice to Daniel if you see him.'

Freya let that comment slide past, but she thought about it as she was carrying the boxes out to the car. Her grandmother really did like Daniel. And she'd missed him not coming by the house.

*Because of her?* Was *she* the reason he

hadn't dropped by in over a week? She reversed out of the narrow parking space. Maybe she was being over-sensitive and he was simply busy sorting out his business. Or his daughter? Either one needed lots of attention. But perhaps she *was* the reason.

The valuation had arrived as promised. Badly typed. Pushed through the letterbox when he could easily have rung the doorbell.

She took the final corner and drove straight onto the auction house forecourt, as close to the central doors as possible, in case she needed to carry the boxes in by herself.

Daniel's daughter was sitting on the wall, her shoulders hunched against the cold, and she had the kind of vacant expression that suggested she wasn't thinking of anything much.

Freya reached forward and turned off the engine. It was *Tuesday* morning. Surely Mia was skipping school, and yet sitting on a wall where her father would see her? Which meant what?

She picked her handbag off the passenger seat and opened the driver's door. A icy January wind blew across the forecourt and she paused to button up her coat, aware that Mia's eyes had turned to watch her, almost as though she wanted to talk.

After the briefest hesitation, Freya walked towards her. 'Hi again.'

Mia hunched a shoulder in recognition.

'Aren't you cold, sitting out here?'

'No.'

And then she shivered, which made Freya want to smile. 'It's freezing. Mind, last time I was here I thought it was as cold inside as out.'

A spark of interest lit Mia's tawny eyes. 'Dad said you said that.' And then, 'He's put a heater in the office now.'

*Had he?* Freya tucked a rogue strand of hair behind her ear. 'Has he forced that window open by any chance?'

Mia almost smiled. Almost, but not quite. 'He took a penknife to it.'

'Excellent! Did it work?'

'Yes, but he broke the penknife.'

Freya laughed.

Mia fingers worked at the frayed cord of her coat. 'You haven't asked why I'm not at school.'

'Why would I? It's none of my business.'

Mia looked up, the expression on her face hovering somewhere between surprise and defiance. 'Everyone does.'

'Oh.'

'I've been expelled. For slapping another girl and swearing at a teacher,' she added, when her first statement didn't elicit the response she'd wanted.

'That would do it.' Freya watched confusion flicker across Mia's eyes. She'd have said she wasn't particularly good with teenagers — she didn't have much experience of them — but she understood this one. However brash Mia sounded, whatever she said, Freya knew she wasn't feeling very 'big' on the inside.

'Dad's really angry.'

She could imagine. 'That's his job.'

There was a sudden spark of laughter in Mia's eyes. They were so like Daniel's when they did that it was a little startling. 'He said that.' The laughter faded and her fingers resumed their picking. 'He says I've ruined my life.'

'What do you think?'

Mia shrugged, and Freya waited. It was the weirdest sensation to know so clearly what was going on in someone else's mind. Or at least to think she did. She could see the fear and hear the need for reassurance in the teenager's voice. 'I don't think it matters.'

'If you've ruined your life?'

Mia shrugged again. 'There are no jobs anyway. You're better off on benefits.'

'You think?' There must have been something in her voice, because Mia looked up curiously. 'It's hard to manage on benefits, you know. Boring when you can't afford to go out. Can't afford to buy the clothes you want. Difficult to find a place to live . . .' She let the thought hang between them for a moment or two.

'School's more boring.'

Freya looked up at the grey clouds moving towards them. 'Whatever your dad said, you've not ruined your life. He knows that. You've just made it more difficult for yourself.' She smiled. 'And he knows that, too. It's probably why he's so angry. Is he here?'

'Somewhere.' Mia nodded towards the building behind her. 'Probably the office.'

'I'd better go and find him. Are you coming in?'

She shook her head. 'He told me to wait out here for my tutor to arrive.' Then, as Freya started to move away, 'Were you expelled ever?'

She'd been waiting for that question. Freya shook her head, inwardly smiling as she saw the teenager's disappointment. 'I wasn't there often enough.'

'You skived?'

'Waited at the same bus stop you were at the other day and took myself to Olban.'

Mia's mouth quirked. 'Aunt Sophy said you were always in trouble.'

*Did she?* Well, there was no surprise there. Freya fought back a stinging reply. Sophia Jameson was Mia's aunt, and she'd respect that.

'Not so much. I was more on a mission to self-destruct. I didn't like school.'

'I hate it.'

'I didn't like my home much, either,' Freya said, watching for a reaction. 'I was really angry. Lonely. I suppose I kind of wanted everyone around me to feel as badly as I was, but I didn't physically hurt anyone. Swore a bit. Drank too much.'

For a moment she thought Mia was about to reply, and then something pulled her gaze away. Freya turned to see Daniel walking towards them. He looked tired, which wasn't so very surprising. With Mia having been expelled, he must have had one hell of a week.

'I'm still here, if you're checking on me,' Mia said, her voice belligerent.

Freya looked back. The change in the teenager was dramatic. Her body was hunched, and the life she'd coaxed out of her had vanished completely.

Daniel wisely ignored the challenge in his daughter's voice and came to a stop beside them. 'Hello.'

'Hi.' *Was it her voice sounding so breathy?* 'I've brought some things down for the general sale. China, mainly. And some old enamelware.'

'Okay.'

Freya moistened her dry lips with the tip of her tongue. This felt so embarrassing. Though goodness only knew why. This was an auction house, and she'd brought something to sell. Nothing embarrassing about that. And yet . . . it was. Really was. That kind of toe-curling embarrassment she remembered from her adolescence.

It felt a whole lot like the way she'd felt when she'd just happened to be outside the Army Cadet hut at twenty past nine each Thursday night, when Calum Dane was leaving.

Only she wasn't fifteen any more; she was nearly thirty. And Daniel Ramsay was no Calum Dane. Even tired, with deep, deep frown lines at the centre of his forehead, he was entirely too gorgeous for a place like Fellingham.

'It's in the car.' Freya moved across to open the passenger door of her car, and went to lift out the box nearest to her.

'Let me see,' Daniel said.

She stood back and watched as he pulled

a penknife — presumably a new one — from his pocket, and scored down the tape she'd placed across the top. 'It's china. Pretty horrible, really.'

He lifted out one of the coffee cups wedged in at the side and carefully unwrapped it. 'That's not horrible. It's Royal Doulton —'

'It says that on the bottom,' Freya cut in. 'I looked.'

Daniel smiled across at her, and her stomach reacted by doing a kind of belly flop. She glanced over at Mia, wondering if the teenager had noticed that one smile from her dad had her hyperventilating.

Since Matt — the male half of her last serious relationship — had packed his bags and left, she'd struggled to summon up much enthusiasm even to date. So what was this? Maybe it was the total abstinence decision which was making Daniel so particularly attractive? The 'you want what you can't have' syndrome?

'It's a nice-quality set. How much of it is there?'

'I've no idea. I didn't count. Sorry. There are teaplates, and a teapot . . .'

His smile broadened, and she fought against inanely smiling back. He had a great smile. It changed his face completely.

Incredibly sexy.

'Let's get it inside, then, and find out. Bob, can you manage the other two?' he asked, calling across to the porter she'd met on her last visit, who'd come to stand in the open doorway.

The older man disappeared for a moment, and then ambled over with a trolley. 'Shall I take that one?'

'No need — I've got it.' Daniel shifted the box in his arms and then started towards the building. 'Mia, give it another five minutes and then you come back in.'

For all the notice his daughter took he might not have spoken. A surreptitious glance in his direction showed he felt it. All signs of laughter had vanished.

Freya helped Bob put the boxes on the trolley, and then paused to lock the door of her car. 'See you later,' she said, looking over at Mia.

She gave a small nod of recognition. Not much, but it was so much more than she'd given her father. Freya pulled her handbag high onto her shoulder and walked slowly inside.

Her grandmother's box of china was already set out on one of the trestle tables, and Daniel had begun to unwrap some of the pieces.

'There's a lot here,' Daniel said as she approached.

'She bought it all in one of the knick-knack places on Beadnell High Street a few years ago, and it's sat in a cupboard unused ever since.'

'Not that surprising,' Daniel said, putting down one of the small coffee cups. 'Almost everyone prefers the convenience of a mug these days. That'll be the trouble with selling this. How much did she pay for it?'

'I've no idea. I'm not sure she even remembers.' Freya watched his long fingers tap against the side of the box.

'I'm happy to sell it for her, but it won't bring as much as you might expect. It's the same with all those wonderful bone-handled cutlery sets. No one wants them any more. They don't fit our twenty-first-century dishwasher lifestyle.'

Freya tucked a strand of blonde hair behind her ear. 'She's got a couple of sets of those, too. Actually, no,' she corrected herself. 'She's got three sets, but one's so tiny it must be for children.'

'That'll be a dessert set,' Daniel said. 'They're difficult to sell, too. The days of cutting up our bananas with a knife and fork have gone.'

He drew his penknife across the tape that

shut the second box. 'This'll be more popular,' he said, lifting out an old enamel flour bin. 'It's not going to make big money, but it's the kind of thing people like in a country kitchen.'

'She really does just want shot of it all.'

Daniel flipped the lid shut. 'Fair enough. We can do that for her. Come through to the office and fill out the paperwork for this lot.'

He really did seem like a man under pressure. Freya slipped her hands into the pockets of her coat and followed him through to his office.

It still had a dank, cold smell about it, but, as Mia had said, it had a heater pumping out hot air. Her eyes wandered up to the grimy window, and she noticed the flaked paint chipped off at the edges.

She looked back and caught Daniel watching her. Faint colour stained his cheekbones, as though he knew what she was thinking.

'Mia said you tried to open it.'

'I thought I'd better see if I could get some ventilation in here, since we're using the fire.'

'Good idea, if Mia's got to work with her tutor in here.'

His eyes narrowed speculatively, and then

he turned away. 'I'll just get you a form to fill in.'

Freya watched as he took a grey box file down from a shelf and walked back with it to the desk. 'How long has Mia been expelled for?'

His hands hesitated before he flipped open the front cover. 'Is that what she said? That she'd been expelled?'

'Yes.'

'She told you?'

Freya nodded. 'Shouldn't she have?'

He turned and pulled a hand across the back of his neck, as though that would ease some of his tension. He exhaled slowly. 'She seems almost proud of it.'

'I don't think that.'

'It's not official yet,' he said quietly. 'At least not in the sense that it's still got to be rubber-stamped by the governing body.'

'Will they?'

'Yes.' Daniel took out a new pad of paper and flicked over the first page. 'Oh, yes. We've got a meeting next Tuesday, to discuss the way forward, but, to be honest, there really isn't one.'

Freya said nothing, just watched the expressions passing over his face. His voice was resigned, but she didn't believe he felt like that for a moment.

'It's possible she might be offered a place in a PRU, but she says she won't go.' He reached for a pen. 'That's a Pupil Referral Unit.'

Freya nodded.

'God only knows what she thinks she's going to do now.'

'Maybe she'll be better for a break. At least . . .' She stopped, searching for the words. 'It's possible that once she sees there aren't a lot of options without exam results she'll want to go back to school.'

'Is that what happened to you?' The question shot from his mouth and pooled in the silence. 'I'm sorry — that's none of my business. I —'

'Of sorts.' Freya bit her lip. She wanted to help. Both of them. She did. But what could she say? Her path wasn't a prescribed one. She'd worked incredibly hard, seen an opportunity and made the most of it, but she'd been lucky.

If she ever had a daughter she wouldn't want her to make the same choices. She'd want what Daniel probably wanted for his daughter — safe choices.

'My sister-in-law told me you left before your exams. I just wondered if —' He spoke into the silence and then stopped abruptly. 'I'm sorry — that was rude question, and also absolutely none of my business.'

For days she'd been dodging questions about what she'd done since she'd left Fellingham, and it was no one's business but her own. But Daniel's motivation for asking was different.

'I did,' she said calmly. 'Well, I left when I was seventeen. But I hadn't turned up for most of my exams the year before, and I dropped out of my retakes.'

'Did you go back later?'

'If I'd needed to I would have. When I had to find somewhere to live, food to eat, everything made more sense to me.'

She watched a muscle pulse in his cheek. Freya searched for words that would describe the . . . *drive* she'd found to succeed. 'I was lucky, but if I hadn't been I know I'd have enrolled myself at college and started over. Mia's too clever not to do the same.'

He pulled a hand across his face.

'I know it's not what you want for her, but she'll surprise you in the end.'

'Did she tell you why she's been expelled?' he asked, handing her the pen.

'She said she slapped a girl.'

'And she would have done a whole lot more if a teacher hadn't been there to pull her off. Completely unprovoked.'

Freya frowned. She doubted that. Mia

didn't come across as someone who was naturally violent. At least not violent without provocation.

In her first squat she'd known a girl who'd had a chip on her shoulder that meant she despised the whole world. She'd been violent simply because of the turmoil going on inside. But that wasn't Mia. She was sure of it.

Freya accepted the pen. 'Did Mia tell you that?'

'Hardly. She doesn't talk. Her mouth was wired together about two months after she turned fourteen.'

*Then how did he know what she'd intended?* He might love his daughter, but he was a good deal too ready to accept other people's evaluation of her.

'Difficult to help her if she won't tell me what the problem is.'

*Impossible.* But . . . he was her dad, and it was his job to try and work out what was eating Mia alive. And, if he wanted her opinion, she'd begin with the death of her mother. It was a screamingly obvious place to start.

But he was unlikely to want her opinion. He rubbed at his right temple, as though there were a sharp pain there, and Freya experienced an overwhelming sadness —

for him and his daughter.

'You need to fill in one of these,' Daniel said, indicating the form on the desk. 'Basically your name and address at the top there. Then a brief description of what you're selling. And whether you'd like us to post a cheque or come in to collect your money.'

'I may as well collect it.'

'Or I can drop it in when I'm passing,' he suggested. He paused while she looked at the form. 'How's Margaret?'

'Sad not to have seen you.'

'I've been busy with Mia.'

Freya looked up. 'Yes.' *Of course he had.* 'Other than that, she's still determinedly packing. We must have filled fifteen or so boxes over the past few days.'

'All destined for here?'

'Mostly. A couple are full of books. I'm not sure what to do with them.' Freya tried to write her surname in the first space, and then drew a couple of circles on the top of the page. 'I'm sorry — I don't think this works.'

Daniel took the pen and aimed it at the wastebin, scoring a direct hit. 'Try this one,' he said, reaching for another pen.

'Thanks.' Freya bent over the desk and filled in details for the first two boxes. 'I'm assuming you want me to put my name in here?'

'It has to be your name if you're going to sign the form. There's a place towards the bottom to say you're bringing in the goods for a third party and want the money to be released to them.'

Freya nodded, and continued on down the form.

'You're welcome to sit down.'

'This won't take a minute,' she said, trying to remember whether the postcode ended with a B or an F. She settled on F.

Beside her, Daniel shut the box file and returned it to the shelf. Freya glanced over, noting the way his denim jeans clung to his beautiful male bottom.

*Whatever had made her think that?* Freya sucked in a breath with lungs that suddenly seemed less effective, and looked back down at the form. Honestly, if Daniel lived in London she'd have been seriously tempted to break her 'no men' resolution.

'Done it,' she said, moments later. 'At least I think I have. I've just put "floral tea service".'

Daniel came closer, and she caught a waft of soap. And the smell of damp cotton hanging about his clothes. It was bizarrely sexy. His arm brushed against hers, and her breath caught as though on cobwebs. She brushed her hair out of her eyes and tried to smile.

This was just the strangest experience. It was a little like walking along a sandy beach and having the tide tug at your toes. Every time she looked at him she felt as though she were sinking a little deeper, becoming more trapped.

Freya blinked hard and stepped back a couple of paces, ready to leave as soon as she possibly could.

'That's great.' He quickly added 'Royal Doulton' next to her description, and then said, 'You just need to sign at the bottom.'

What did Daniel think about her? She just couldn't tell. There were moments when she thought there might be *something,* but most of the time he appeared oblivious. Which was good.

Probably.

Freya took two steps back towards the table.

'Just here,' he said, pointing.

She bent over the table and put her signature on the dotted line.

'That's everything. I'll put the cheque through the door some time.' The door banged behind him and he turned, leaving Freya to return the pen to the chipped mug.

The porter was there, holding on to the handle. 'Chris Lewis has come to deliver that office furniture. Do you want me to tell him to bring his van right in?'

Daniel looked at her, his brown eyes holding a glint of unexpected laughter. 'Do you need to get out first?'

Her stomach reacted predictably. 'Probably.'

'Tell him to hang on a minute. I'll —' He broke off as his phone rang. 'I'm sorry — I have to get this.'

She nodded. 'Ramsay Auctioneers.' A short pause and then, 'Jack!'

Freya looked across at the porter. She ought to go while he was busy. Run while she had the chance. Go back and continue with the packing. 'Is that everything I need to do?'

'You've filled out the sheet, have you, love?'

She nodded and pointed down at the table. 'All done.'

'That's it, then,' he said, coming into the room and letting the door bang shut behind him.

Freya looked across at Daniel, meaning to point at the door as a kind of farewell gesture, but he was looking down at his watch.

'I can't do anything before midday. Mia's got a tutor coming today, and there has to be a responsible adult present.'

Daniel stepped back and his elbow caught a large pile of papers, which scattered over the floor. Freya crouched down and automatically started to pick them up.

He mouthed his thanks and spoke into the phone. 'The agency couldn't send anyone again today. And even if they could I don't think I could leave Mia with them. That's not exactly in the job description.'

Freya looked up as she placed a brown manila file on the desk. Her eyes met his and he gave something approaching a shrug, as though he could guess what she was thinking about the chaos of his life.

She smiled, and gathered together a loose selection of papers. It did look hellish — but that wasn't what she was thinking. In her entire life she'd never felt this kind of connection to someone, a feeling that their problems mattered to her simply because they were theirs. If that made any sense.

There was absolutely no reason for her to be concerned about his relationship with his daughter. Or the way he ran his business. Or the fact he didn't have enough hours in the day to be in all the places he needed to be.

*Except she liked him.*

How scary was that? She could cope with finding a man sexually attractive. That was a biological response. But to *like* someone was something else entirely. It suggested an emotional connection — and that terrified her.

Freya settled the last of the papers on the desk and then turned as she felt a waft of cold air. A woman, conservatively dressed, with neatly bobbed hair, walked confidently into the office with Mia beside her. The door banged shut.

'I'm Susan Phillips. Mia's home tutor.'

Freya glanced back at Daniel. He pulled a hand across the back of his neck and she fought the desire to walk over and hold him. He looked like a man who needed a hug.

'You'll need to have a word with Mia's dad. He won't be a minute.'

'Look, I'm going to have to go,' Daniel said into the receiver. 'I'll call you back in five minutes.' There was a pause, during which he raked the same hand through his hair. 'I know. I'm sorry, but it can't be helped. Right. Yes. Bye.' He put the phone down and immediately turned his attention to the tutor. 'I'm so sorry.'

'Daniel Ramsay?'

'Yes.'

'I'm Susan Phillips.'

'Hello. Yes, we were expecting you.'

Freya was pushed back against the table as the door opened again and a large man stood in the gap. The already over-filled office seemed to shrink a few feet more. 'Do I get to bring the van in? It's blocking the road.'

It was chaos. A type that would have been unimaginable in her tightly controlled offices.

Daniel spared her the briefest of glances, and then turned towards the man in the doorway. 'Hang on. I'll be with you in a minute —'

'Don't worry,' Freya said quietly. 'It's fine. I'll wait until you've finished unloading.' That part was easy. 'I've got nothing I need to rush off to today,' she said by way of explanation as Daniel turned to look at her.

She wasn't at all sure whether it was part of the home tutor's remit to report back on the home situation, but if it was then this wasn't the best of starts. Mia looked sulky, and entirely disengaged from the whole proceedings. Daniel looked like someone who was being pushed further than he could manage.

'Okee-dokee,' the porter said cheerfully. He ushered the larger man out of the room.

'I'll get a couple of lads to help you with the desks and such.'

Daniel waited until the door had swung shut behind them before turning back to his daughter's tutor. 'A delivery of office furniture has arrived. A little earlier than we'd anticipated.'

Ms Phillips didn't seem remotely interested, merely unbuttoning the top button of her coat. 'We ought to get started. Is there a quiet place we can work?'

Freya hung back. *She could help him.* It would be so easy. She just had to offer. It didn't have to mean anything. And it wouldn't be for long.

'I thought here,' Daniel said, looking at the desk in the corner.

The tutor's mouth pursed slightly. 'We will need quiet in order to concentrate.'

It wasn't so much what she said as the way that she said it. Freya felt her own ire rising at the aggressive stance she'd adopted.

'There's a small kitchenette and a table through there,' Daniel said, pointing at a door in the far left-hand corner, 'but I honestly think you'd be better off in here. Mia and I cleared a space earlier this morning.'

Susan Phillips slipped of her coat. 'We can try,' she said, sounding as though she'd offered a great concession. 'I assume there'll be a responsible adult staying throughout?'

Daniel hesitated. The first time since Susan Phillips had blown into the auction house.

Freya stopped agonising and just acted. 'That would be me.'

Daniel's head swung round in complete disbelief, his eyes unreadable. All of a sudden she wanted to laugh. Freya tossed her hair and set her bag down on the table. 'I'm staying to chaperon.'

# CHAPTER SIX

*What the — ?* Daniel raked a hand through his hair. What was Freya doing now? He caught the edge of her smile before she turned back to Mia's tutor.

'Mia's father has an unexpected appointment this morning, so I'm staying in his place.'

'I see.'

Beside him Freya slipped off her jacket and reached out a hand to take the tutor's grey-coloured raincoat. 'Where shall I hang these?' she asked, turning to him.

This was like stepping into an alternate universe. Better than the one he'd inhabited up to now, but certainly different. He'd decided Freya Anthony was a temptation best avoided. For all kinds of reasons. All good. But here she was, offering him a lifeline he couldn't exactly refuse.

*But why was she doing it?*

'Daniel?' she prompted.

He must look like an idiot. 'Just here,' he said, moving past her and shutting the door to reveal a row of four hooks.

'Have you got a hanger?'

'No.'

One beautifully shaped eyebrow flicked up, and he knew exactly what she was thinking. *She'd* have several hangers. A window that opened. Ergonomically designed office furniture arranged on feng shui principles.

Despite everything, he felt like laughing. She walked over and carefully slid the loop of the tutor's dark coat over the first hook.

'What are you doing?' he murmured quietly.

She looked up, and he almost forgot what he'd asked. Wide blue eyes met his. 'Helping.'

Daniel took her jacket from her hands and slid the loop over the next hook along, taking the opportunity to say quietly, 'This is going to be at least an hour.'

'That's fine.'

*Fine?* This was the woman who, less than two weeks ago, hadn't been prepared to wait twenty minutes. So why . . . ? What . . . ?

If she were the kind of woman Sophy thought her, then he was hardly an obvious target for her attention. He'd got no money to speak of, and responsibilities coming out of every pore.

'Freya?' he breathed, as she was about to turn away.

She glanced over her shoulder, her incredible eyes full of mischief. 'Yes?'

With Mia's tutor standing so close he couldn't have the conversation he wanted with her — and she knew it, and was enjoying every second. He pulled a hand through his hair and watched helplessly as she walked back into the centre of the room.

'Can I get you a coffee or tea before you start work?'

'Coffee would be lovely. Thank you.' The tutor managed something approaching a smile, but it was still fairly tight-lipped. 'White, no sugar.'

'Perhaps Mia and I could get that?' Freya suggested, looking at his daughter. 'You could show me where everything is, and your dad could check with Ms Phillips that she has everything she needs.'

Mia didn't answer, but she slid down from the low sideboard on which she'd been perched and walked towards the kitchenette. Considering she'd been fairly vocal earlier about not wanting to do any kind of schoolwork, this was a major step forward.

'I'm not sure this room will be suitable long-term, Mr Ramsay,' the tutor said, pulling his attention back to her. 'In fact, I've got reservations about trying to teach here at all. If we have too many distractions today we'll have to have a major rethink.'

The door to the kitchenette clicked shut, and he felt more able to concentrate on what the older woman was saying. 'Of course.'

'Is there no one at home who could chaperon?'

'Not since my wife died. No.'

Usually people fell over themselves to offer their sympathy, but Ms Phillips was made of sterner stuff. A frown snapped across her forehead. 'Perhaps it would be possible for your receptionist to go there . . . ?'

'Freya's not my receptionist. She's a friend of a friend who has offered to help out on this occasion.'

'I see.'

She didn't, because he didn't, either. *Was Freya doing this for him?* It didn't make any sense. Unless she was doing it for Mia.

That was possible. But he didn't like the idea as much as he preferred the one which put *him* centre stage.

Susan swung round and looked at the desk he'd carefully cleared earlier. 'I think that will probably be best for our purposes.'

'Right.'

'And perhaps your friend would sit in the room off here? I'd prefer it if we had this room to ourselves. I find the students concentrate more if they don't have anyone else to play to. But of course we'll need to leave the door ajar.'

What she said made sense, but his thoughts immediately went to the window-less kitchenette Freya would have to sit in.

Susan Phillips settled herself in the chair to one side of the desk, looking up at him with a slightly irritated expression and a swift glance at the wall clock. 'As soon as Mia's ready we'll get started.'

'I'll fetch her.' Daniel walked over to the door and opened it.

He wasn't sure what he'd expected to find. From what he could tell Mia had decided she liked Freya, but whether she had enough 'pull' to get her to co-operate with schoolwork was another matter.

'Ms Phillips would like to get started,' he said, watching as his daughter poured milk into the two cups on the table. *How was it everything had gone so wrong?*

Freya stood up and took the milk carton from Mia's hand. 'I'll put this away. The sooner you get started, the sooner you'll be done.' She walked over to the fridge and opened the door.

His daughter pulled a face, but she picked up the mug and a glass of water for herself.

'Don't blow this,' he said, unable to stop himself, and winced as she let the door slam shut behind her. *Damn!* He didn't need the flick of Freya's expressive eyebrows to tell him that hadn't been clever. 'I know. Stupid to say it.'

'She won't blow it.'

'You reckon?'

Freya just smiled, but she hadn't been around to see the chances Mia had already thrown away. He glanced down at his watch.

'Are you sure about this? If you want to back out now —'

'It's not for long.' She returned to the other side of the table and sat down, cradling one of Anna's hand-thrown mugs in her hands. One of the early ones, made during the time she'd been experimenting with glazes. 'Do I stay in here?'

Daniel nodded. 'I'm sorry.'

'I offered. Actually —' her smile widened '— I didn't give you much choice.'

'Why?'

'Because I can. Because it's a nice thing to do. Because if I go home and say I didn't my life won't be worth living.'

That reason coaxed a smile out of him.

'And you know I'm right.' Freya sipped her coffee, her eyes watchful above the rim.

'If you're sure . . . ?'

'Are you always this difficult to help? Make your call, do what you need to do, and come back when you've finished. This is a piece of nothing.'

*Just like that.* For the first time since he'd met her he could see something of Margaret in her. That same determined tilt of the chin, and the same laughter hidden deep in the dark blue of her eyes. She knew he was finding it hard to accept help, and there was a part of her that was really enjoying that.

Truth be told, he'd have been a darn sight more comfortable with the whole thing if it were Margaret sitting there. Freya came with baggage, for want of a better word. Certainly a poor reputation — and, while he preferred to take as he found, he wasn't at all sure he wanted too much interaction between her and his daughter.

But what choice had he? Daniel pulled his hand through his hair, easing his fingers across the sharp pain at the base of his skull. 'I'll pay you for your time.'

The twinkle in her eyes deepened. 'Just go. We can talk about that later.'

'Thank you.'

'Go!'

Daniel pulled his mobile from his pocket. 'I've got this switched on if you need me.'

Freya nodded.

'Mia knows the number.'

She laughed.

Daniel felt the tension ease from his shoulders. 'Okay, I'm going.'

Daniel swung his estate car into the auction forecourt, half expecting to see Freya's car gone. Two hours was too long.

*Damn it!* He should have phoned. No, actually, he should have just come back to coincide with the end of the tutoring session. If Freya was madly tapping her foot he'd only have himself to blame.

And goodness only knew what kind of mood Mia would be in. He'd promised to take her up to Stotfold Farm so she could go riding with Sophy this afternoon . . .

He slammed the door of his car. The fact he'd discovered a veritable treasure trove shouldn't have been a factor.

'Mia? Freya?' Daniel called. He pushed open the door of the office and immediately saw the two of them laughing, surrounded by box files and half opened boxes. He took a moment to take it all in. The reality was completely different from anything he'd been imagining.

His daughter looked up. 'We're sorting through the archives.'

'So I see.'

'Freya can't stand mess.'

Daniel looked across at Freya, with the sleeves of her cashmere jumper pushed up and her blonde hair pulled back in a loose ponytail, soft fronds falling about her face. She looked as if she thought she might have been caught doing something she shouldn't.

'Guilty as charged. Do you mind?'

So much younger than she'd looked the first time he'd met her. Less intimidating, if he was honest. Enchanting. He wasn't sure where *that* thought came from, but it slid into his brain and settled there.

And Mia was happy. Sophy might think she'd be a disastrous influence, but all indications were to the contrary. And since when had he ever rated Sophy's judgement highly?

'Don't let me stop you.'

His daughter stood up and reached for a pad on the table. 'We've taken all the messages. There are a couple of important ones.'

He reached out for the pad, but his eyes were on Freya. Somehow she'd worked a little miracle and he was *beggared* if he knew how.

'Thanks.' He cleared his throat. 'I'm sorry

I'm so much later than I thought.'

'We phoned Margaret so she wouldn't worry,' Mia said. 'And Aunt Sophy to say I'd be late for riding. Freya says people get less irritated if they know what's happening.'

Daniel winced. 'I should have phoned you.'

'We had your number if we wanted to call you. We were fine. Warm,' Freya said, in a voice full of soft laughter.

His daughter brushed dust off her jodhpurs. 'This place is really dirty, though.'

'When we've cleared the floor you can mop it.'

Mia held out a pair of grubby hands. 'Cool.'

A real miracle. Daniel watched as the miracle-worker closed a wallet folder and set it on the pile to her left. As though she felt his gaze, she looked up — and then she smiled.

There was a whole movie industry built around the power of that kind of smile. It was just a smile, and yet it wasn't. Sudden wanting swept through him. He hardly knew her — knew there were a thousand and one reasons why it was better things stayed that way — but for the first time in years he felt — Just that. *Felt.* Something. Anything.

He'd spent years now in a kind of limbo.

A kind of nothingness. He woke up, he went to bed, and in the middle he got on with things. But in the space of a moment he knew he wanted more than that. He wanted her.

He pulled his gaze away and transferred it to his daughter. That was where his attention should be focused. All the time. On Mia.

Anna would expect that. He'd promised her he'd take care of their daughter. *Promised her.* And that promise didn't include taking time out to get involved with a woman she probably hadn't liked.

'I can take you up to the farm now. I'll get Bob to listen out for the phone.'

'But we've not finished,' Mia said, her eyes travelling over the controlled chaos.

Whilst he was thrilled to see this embryonic sense of responsibility, he really wanted to be gone. He wanted to shut the door on all this and think about what was happening to him. Somehow, in the space of a few minutes, everything had shifted for him — and he really didn't like it. 'It'll all still be here later.'

'But it's sorted. It just needs putting away.'

He hadn't seen Mia so engaged in anything for the longest time. Daniel put his hands deep into his long wax coat and straightened his spine a fraction. He was out of his depth here, and entirely uncertain what he should do.

In his peripheral vision he saw Freya get up from her knees. She straightened her wrap-around jumper across her breasts and smoothed out her black trousers.

*What had Anna thought of her twelve years ago? What would she have thought now?*

'How would it be if I stayed to make sure we don't go backwards and you go off riding?' Freya smiled over at Mia.

'There's no need —' he began, but the lift of an eyebrow silenced him. He was beginning to sound like a broken record even in his own ears. What possible excuse could he give that wouldn't sound lame? She was offering to sort out his paperwork, not move into his home and fill it with cupcakes.

He smoothed out the tension in the back of his neck. 'Are you sure Margaret can manage without you?'

'She's out at the Women's Institute fundraiser. I'm better off here.'

*Fellingham's very own 'bad girl'* — and he was falling for her hook, line and sinker. Did Freya know that? And, if she did, how did she feel about it?

Mia reached for her jumper, which had been draped over the back of a chair, and pulled it over her head. 'As long as we don't have to start from the beginning again, I'm cool. It's taken way too long.' She looked at Freya. 'Shall we finish this tomorrow?'

Freya looked across at Daniel, a slight question now in those beautiful dark-lashed eyes. It said, *What do you want?*

*And he didn't know.* If it were just the offer of some reliable office help that would be easy — but it wasn't. Not for him, even if it were for her.

'Freya's here to help Margaret,' he said lamely.

'I can manage a couple of hours a day,' Freya said, looking directly at him. 'If it'll help? Perhaps we could combine it with Mia's tutor's visits, and that'll free you up too?'

*Two hours every day.* He'd see her every day. And then one day she'd leave. She'd go back to her glamorous London life. The kind that required soft suede jackets the colour of clotted cream and high suede boots.

How would he feel then?

*And what about the alternative?* What if she stayed? In Anna's house? With Anna's daughter? *With him?*

Daniel pulled his car keys from his pocket. 'If you're going riding, I'd better take you up to Sophy's now. There's no need to stay if you need to get away,' he said, risking a look at Freya. 'Bob'll mind the phones.'

Her smile dimmed, and he immediately felt awful. Her eyelids hid the expression in her eyes, but he knew he'd hurt her. His hands balled into fists by his sides.

*He was making a mess of this. Something else he was making a mess of.*

'I'm feeling really awkward about all this.' He pulled the words out. 'I'm completely wrecking your day. Your stay with Margaret . . .'

'Actually, I love doing things like this.'

She smiled, and he felt his chest grow tight. Was she really trying to convince him he was doing her the favour? Daniel forced his fingers to relax.

'My plans are really fluid, but I'm going to be here another couple of weeks at least.'

*Two weeks wasn't long.* He wasn't sure whether that was a good thing or a bad thing. From the hard ache in the centre of his chest he was inclined to think it fell more on the side of 'bad thing'.

'Are we going, then?'

Daniel turned his head to look at Mia. 'Have you got everything you need?'

'I left my stuff up at Aunt Sophy's.'

'Okay, then. Let's go.'

'See you tomorrow, Freya,' Mia said,

opening the door.

*Two weeks of Freya Anthony in his life. How did he feel about that?*

# CHAPTER SEVEN

Freya slipped an invoice for January into its proper place and shut the file. She loved this. She really did. Creating order out of chaos was balm to her soul. Right from a little girl, she'd loved setting everything to rights.

More unexpected was that she genuinely liked being in this place. She liked the steady tick of the old station clock on the wall by the door, the smell of . . . She sniffed. She wasn't exactly sure what the smell was. It was a kind of mustiness, but not quite and not unpleasant.

She lifted the box file and went to put it back on the high shelf she'd assigned to it. She liked knowing she was being useful, too. Without even thinking about it she could find things to do which would keep her busy for months.

Two weeks she'd told Daniel — and that was about right. Long enough to do some good. Short enough to do no harm.

Freya picked up a second box file to return it to the shelf and then hesitated as she heard voices some way in the distance. She set the box on the shelf and turned in time to see the door open.

'You're still here.'

'I've just got those to put up here,' she said, indicating the eight box files on the floor, 'and then I think I'm done for today.'

*Who was she kidding?* Two weeks was plenty of time to wreak havoc. Seeing him was like being kicked in the solar-plexus. And it was so unexpected. Daniel looked like a living personification of *Country Living* magazine — wax jacket, snug jeans, hair crisply curling from the damp air outside.

Up to now she'd thought she was a city girl through and through, but there was something incredibly seducing about it all. Sexy.

But then with or without the wax jacket Daniel was sexy. Something about his eyes, she reckoned. The crinkle at the corner which made her want to smile back. Or maybe it was the frown at the centre of his forehead that made her want to smooth the lines out with her finger.

He shrugged out of his jacket and threw it over the newly cleared desk. 'This looks amazing. You've done a great job.'

For someone who'd created a successful business from tiny beginnings that shouldn't have meant as much to her as it did. 'It's going to look better than this.'

His eyes narrowed, then he thrust his hands deep into the pockets of jeans. 'I thought you didn't want this job.'

'I don't,' she said quickly. 'Not as a job.'

'Then why do this?'

She drew a shallow breath. *Because you need my help. Because I like you. Because I can.* The answers were easy to find, less easy to say. 'Why not?'

The frown lines above the bridge of his nose deepened. 'If it clashes with anything else you've got planned you need to say.'

'Of course.'

Daniel picked up a couple of the box files and carried them over to her. 'I could pay you what I do the agency. That way it'll be a bit above the going rate.'

'You don't —'

'This is a deal-breaker.' He turned to look at her. 'The fact you're prepared to chaperon Mia if needed is worth a lot. Obviously I'll try and be here, but . . .' He shrugged. 'A safety net would be great. I'd appreciate that.'

Was this the moment she ought to tell him

just how much she didn't need his money? The words hovered on the tip of her tongue and then she swallowed them back down.

If she did it would change things, and she didn't want that. Since Matt had left all the men she'd dated had only dollar and pound signs when they looked at her. Matt hadn't been able to cope with her success. Wealth, she'd discovered, was something of a poisoned chalice. A bit disheartening when it had been her *raison d'être* for a decade.

Freya walked back and picked up another file. He might not even like to feel she was helping because she felt sorry for him. And, actually, she didn't. He wasn't the kind of man you could feel pity for. She just felt an overwhelming sadness for the circumstances in which he found himself.

'Okay,' she said slowly. 'I'll keep some kind of timesheet. That way we can be a bit flexible about it all.' There was a small pause. 'So we have a deal?'

'I think we do.'

Somewhere, not so far to the back of her mind, alarm bells were screeching as he held out his hand. This wasn't wise. She liked him. She might even be falling in love with him. And everything about Daniel was wrong for her.

She stretched out her own hand and let

his fingers close round hers. For once she didn't think about whether her hand was on top or beneath. It didn't enter her head to take the dominant position or control the length of the handshake.

His hand felt good round hers. Warm and strong. Her eyes flew up to his face — anywhere to avoid looking at the contrast of her pale skin and his darker hand.

But his eyes were the wrong place to look. The air between them crackled with something she didn't understand and hadn't experienced before. Her breath came in painful gasps and her head felt as if a tight iron band had been wrapped round it. It was a lot like she imagined jumping off a cliff would feel. Exhilarating. Scary.

And she wanted him to kiss her. Every single fibre of her being wanted him to pull her closer. She wanted to know what it would be like to have those hands slide down her back. Her eyes flicked to his lips. She wanted to kiss him. *Really wanted that.*

And for a girl who usually just reached out and took whatever she wanted it was a bizarre feeling to let him release her and turn away. Freya bit down hard on her bottom lip until she could taste blood.

'I ought to be getting back.'

His head turned. She watched the movement of his throat as he swallowed. 'I thought Margaret was at the Women's Institute fundraiser this afternoon?'

'She is. Until three-ish.'

'Then come and get some lunch.'

*With him?*

'I'm going to grab a baguette or something similar at the Wheatsheaf.'

Freya moistened her lips with the tip of her tongue in a nervous gesture. He made it sound like the most casual of all invitations. Heaven help her, she was entirely out of her depth. She wasn't good at this type of thing. Hopelessly out of practice at reading the subtext.

It was probably only a handful of seconds, but it felt longer. 'Okay.'

Daniel walked over to the door. 'Bob, keep an ear out for the phone, will you? I'm on the mobile if you need to get me.'

She hung back while he picked up his coat, pulling the band from her hair and running her fingers through the tousled curls.

'I won't be long,' he said as Bob stuck his head round the door. 'Forty minutes, maybe.'

The older man nodded. Freya deliberately turned away and busied herself by looking in her handbag for her credit card. She felt . . . self-conscious. There was no other way to describe how she was feeling.

Out of her depth and self-conscious — and she'd barely even started to think what it would be like to walk into a pub right in the centre of Fellingham. Had he thought at all about what people would think when they saw them together?

'Okay?' Daniel turned to smile at her, leading the way across the auction house floor and out. 'It's literally round the corner.'

'Yes, I know.' The wind swiped across the forecourt and Freya caught her breath as it blew directly into her face. 'It feels cold enough to snow,' she said, huddling down into the warmth of the sheepskin.

'Possibly.'

Freya nervously filled the silence. 'I'm glad you managed to do something about putting a fire into that office. I think Ms Phillips might have been seen running in the opposite direction if you hadn't.'

'She wasn't that keen to work there anyway.'

Freya struggled to keep pace with his long stride. 'She seemed happy enough in the end.'

'Was she?'

'Well, she didn't mumble anything too

negative at the end. Just said she'd be back on Friday.'

'We were certainly on trial.' He modified his step, suddenly becoming aware that she was almost running. 'Sorry. Mia's always telling me I walk too fast.'

His eyes wandered down to Freya's feet, and the high heels she'd been tripping along beside him in. Real city girl shoes. The kind that were designed to go from penthouse to car to restaurant and back.

Soft mizzle began to fall from the grey sky. Daniel looked up. 'Looks like we're going to be just in time. Perhaps Mia's not going to get her ride after all.'

'Where does she go?'

'Stotfold. The hamlet between Paxton and —'

'Yardley. I know it.'

'Her aunt lives there and has a couple of horses.'

'Sophia?'

'Yes.' You couldn't tell from Freya's voice what she thought of his sister-in-law. Was their dislike mutual? It surely must be.

'She and her ex-husband bought Stotfold Farm.'

'Arthur Cambell's old place?'

'I don't remember. They bought about four acres of the original farm.'

They walked past the newsagents and crossed the road towards the Wheatsheaf. Freya's pace slowed. 'The car park is full.'

'It always is.'

'Really?'

'Always,' he confirmed, looking down at her, suddenly sensing how nervous she was. 'It'll be fine.'

Her blue eyes met his. For a moment he thought she was going to deny feeling any kind of unease, but then her mouth twisted into a half-smile.

'You can't stay hidden away for ever. And you have every right to be here.'

She stamped her foot, as though she were trying to bring life back into cold toes. 'Easy for you to say.'

'Your call.' And then he waited.

She visibly straightened her spine and flicked back her blonde hair. 'I think I'm tired of letting other people control what I do.'

'Then let's do it.'

'The last time I was here I was under-age.'

'Was this a regular haunt?' he asked, stepping up under the porch.

'I didn't come here often. If I wanted to indulge in any kind of illegal drinking I didn't try it closer to home than Olban.'

'Ah.'

'I wasn't stupid. At least not in that sense.'

*Which meant what?* That she regretted the things she'd done? And what exactly were they? The only thing he knew for certain was that she'd left Fellingham with a lad from the local estate. Reports varied as to his name, but all seemed to agree that he'd been several years older and the drummer in a local band.

She pushed the heavy door open and Daniel followed her inside.

'Grief!'

Daniel laughed. 'It's changed a bit. There were one or two complaints when they ripped down the old horse brasses, but pretty much they've managed to keep all of the period features intact and local opinion has come down largely in favour.'

He watched as she scanned the crowded bar area, then took in the careful melding of old and new.

'They've done a good job.' Freya stepped back as a man carrying three pints of beer knocked her arm.

'Sorry, love.'

Instinctively Daniel's hands moved to steady her, coming to rest on her arms. His breath caught as her hair softly brushed against his face, and he was rocked by how protective of her he felt. 'Of course there's a downside to it being popular,' he said, forcing himself to let her go.

The room was humming with conversation, and there were lots of people congregated by the bar, but fortunately there were still some free seats. He made a concerted effort to keep his voice light. 'Any preference as to where we sit?'

'There,' she said, pointing at a couple of sofas tucked into an alcove.

Slightly out of the way. The perfect choice if you wanted to escape too much notice. With real city girl flair Freya cut a swathe across the crowded room and settled herself in the sofa which gave her the best view of the rest of the room.

'If you let me know what you'd like, I'll go and order it at the bar.'

She shrugged out of her jacket and let it fall carelessly beside her on the sofa. Then she crossed her legs, before leaning forward to pick up the creamy coloured menu. 'What are you having?' she asked, looking up.

'I occasionally branch out with a Mexican Chicken baquette, but I've got a bit of an addiction to Spicy Meatball panini.'

Her blue eyes smiled. 'I'll try that, then. And I'd better stay on sparkling water since I've got to drive back.'

'Fine.' Daniel took the menu from her, and then jumped up to place their order.

He'd forgotten how to do this. The casual drink and bar snack. The date that wasn't quite a date, because then there was no pressure and no awkwardness about not doing it again.

*This felt awkward.* And he'd not considered how difficult Freya might find it coming here. She was on the alert. Jumping each time the door opened, relaxing when it wasn't anyone she knew.

He'd meant what he'd said. She had every right to be here. *Damn it,* she'd been seventeen when she'd left Fellingham. She hadn't committed any crime he knew about. People served less time for murder.

He glanced over his shoulder, fascinated to see that she was biting her nails. Something she couldn't often allow herself to do. One of the first things he'd noticed about her was how beautifully manicured her hands were. He smiled as warmth spread through his chest. Outwardly she was so together, so cool, but that was just a veneer. Underneath there were all kinds of emotions bubbling away, and he really wanted to know what they were.

He turned back to the bar and placed his order with the barman, his mind on anything but. He wanted to know everything about her. Why she'd left Fellingham and, more importantly, what had happened to her since.

What was it that had put the sadness in her eyes? Why was she taking a year out when other women her age were hearing the tick of their biological clock? How was it she was driving such an expensive car? Wearing such expensive clothes? Was any of that important to her?

So many questions and so little time to ask them. Freya wouldn't be staying long in Fellingham. Two weeks and she'd be gone. Maybe a little more if Margaret needed her. Not long.

Drinks in hand, he walked back towards her. 'I let them put in ice. I hope that was okay?'

Freya nodded and accepted the long tall glass. 'That's great.'

He set his beer down on a coaster. 'They'll bring the paninis over in a few minutes. It shouldn't be too long.'

'I'm not the one who has to get back to work.'

'True.' He took off his wax coat and threw it over the back of the sofa before sitting down opposite her.

'Do you like what you do?'

Her voice was full of curiosity, as though it were a question she'd wanted to ask for a while. He supposed it wasn't so surprising, considering the state of his business. She was right when she'd said it needed an injection of capital. But more than that it needed his time.

Daniel picked up his beer glass and took a sip. 'Mostly. But right now I could do with the business being about five years further on.'

'How old is it?'

'Four years. But the whole start-up has been difficult.' His thumb brushed against his wedding ring and he twisted the band of metal round. 'My wife . . . Anna died in our first year here.'

She should have had more time. The first round of chemo had been successful. Or so they'd thought. But then the disease had swept in for a second time, with a ferocity that had caught them all by surprise.

'She'd been ill for a long time. But the end came quite suddenly. Not so very long after we'd come here.'

'I'm sorry.'

'It was very hard on Mia.'

'Hard on you both,' she countered. 'Did Mia know her mum was dying?'

'Towards the end. At the point at which

we were told all her treatment was palliative we told her.' Daniel looked down at the beer in his hand and drew his forefinger up the condensation on his glass. 'It gave Anna time to put some things together for Mia. She kept a video diary, wrote letters. That kind of thing.'

Freya watched him swallow. Pain radiated from him, and it was rather beautiful. He'd really loved his wife.

A new wave of loneliness washed over her. If she became sick, if she died, there'd be no one to mourn her. No one for whom she'd made the world a better place on any kind of personal level.

Daniel managed a smile — the kind people gave when they wanted to pretend everything was just fine. 'She hand-made cards for her birthdays, for her engagement, for her wedding . . .' He pulled a hand over his face. 'This is a bit of a heavy conversation for a Tuesday lunchtime. I'm sorry.'

'Don't be.' Freya took a sip of her sparkling water. 'Missing her is the best compliment you can pay her.'

He ran his hand down his thigh. 'I wish she was here to deal with Mia. I'm making a bad job of it.'

It was the opening she'd been waiting for, but now it was here she was strangely reluctant to begin. 'Has Mia spoken to anyone about how she feels about her mum's death?'

Daniel shook his head. 'She didn't want to.'

'Then. What about now?'

He smiled and took a sip of his beer. 'Wouldn't that be simple?' he said dryly.

Freya twisted her earring between her forefinger and thumb. Maybe it was arrogant of her to think she had the answers when he must have spent hours thinking about how to help his daughter.

Only . . . what if she did?

'She's angry.'

'I know that.'

'And she's scared.'

His hand hesitated on the way up to his mouth with the beer glass. 'And you know that how?'

'Because I was scared. I got tagged as trouble but inside I was so frightened.' Freya let her hair fall forwards, so that it hid the deep blush she knew was burning across her face. She was in new territory here. For all she was suggesting Mia talked, *she'd* never talked to anyone about what had happened to her. At least not someone she hadn't been paying to listen.

In a way she was ashamed, because it

didn't seem to be so very much. It wasn't as though she'd been beaten, or sexually abused, or any of the terrible things that hit the headlines. She'd just been unhappy. Desperately unhappy.

Daniel put his glass down on the table. The expression on his face had changed from defensive to attentive. She'd begun this, and now he wanted to know what had happened.

'Of what?'

'Life. My life.' She tried to smile, but it slipped. 'What has Sophia said about me?'

He sat back, looking uncomfortable.

'Don't worry — I know she will have talked to you about me.' She stopped and waited while a group of three women walked out of earshot. 'And I know she doesn't like me.'

'No, she doesn't.'

Freya mouth twisted into a wry smile. There was no prevarication. No platitude.

'She says you liked to be the centre of attention. That you manipulated people and events to suit yourself. You spent all your time smoking and drinking with the lads from the estate —'

'I get the picture.' Maybe Sophia believed what she was saying? Maybe she'd even felt intimidated by her? Freya herself only remembered feeling isolated and frozen out of her peer group.

'Sophy isn't always a good judge of character.'

'I did what I could to show everyone I didn't care what they thought of me. I did do that.' It was funny that Sophia thought she'd wanted to be the centre of attention when all she'd wanted was *some* attention. Behind her eyes she felt a sharp prick of tears, which she blinked away.

'Freya —'

She brushed an irritated hand across her face. 'It's okay. It's why coming to a place like this is difficult. I'm twenty-nine, and I'm still worried about what other people are thinking about me. It's so stupid.'

'We can leave.'

Freya shook her head. 'I wanted this year to be a new start. Maybe I need to really clear away the old stuff before I'm ready for any new beginnings.'

'We could have gone further afield. I didn't think.'

'Why would you? You're *nice.* I suspect everyone has always liked you.'

'Apart from the time I got Professor Jameson's daughter pregnant. I wasn't so very popular then.'

It was weird how close crying and laughter

actually were. One moment she was struggling to keep back the tears and the next she was laughing. 'I imagine that was a fun time.'

Daniel sat back on the sofa. 'Making Mia was fun. Telling Anna's father less so.'

'Why didn't Anna carry on with her university course?'

'She didn't want to.' Daniel took another sip of his beer. 'She'd only gone to uni in the first place because her parents expected it. And she was doing French and Spanish when she'd really wanted to do something art based.'

'Oh?' From the outside Anna Jameson had seemed to have everything. Freya hadn't ever paused to think about the pressure the Professor and his wife had been putting on her. On both their daughters.

Freya looked up as the door opened, helplessly tensing until she saw that the couple who'd walked in were complete strangers to her.

'We can go. Just say the word and we'll leave.'

She shook her head. 'I shouldn't mind so much what people think about me.'

'We all do, to some extent.' There was an edge to his voice which surprised her. His eyes met hers and his mouth twitched into a half smile. Self-deprecating and sexy as hell. 'What do you imagine people are saying about my parenting skills? Every mistake Mia makes they look at me. I hate that.'

He might be surprised. As far as she knew absolutely no one had blamed her parents for any of *her* sins. It had been more a case of 'Poor David and Christine'.

'I know what my grandma thinks.'

Daniel leant forward, resting his elbows on his knees. 'Go on.'

'That you're a nice man, doing the best you can.'

He smiled, but said, 'Not enough, though, is it?' Then he sat back. 'Why were you scared?'

'Because . . .' She searched for the words. 'Because my hormones had kicked in and everything was changing, and I didn't know how to unpack any of it because I was still a child. I didn't feel like a child. But then I wasn't an adult, either.'

He frowned.

'And because everything I thought was safe had started to shift about.' Freya felt a sudden bubble of grief burst inside her. She'd talked about her parents' marriage before, but Dr Coxan hadn't looked at her with the kind of expression Daniel had. He cared.

'Freya, what happened?'

Unshed tears seemed to be blocking her throat, making it difficult to speak. 'Nothing as dreadful as has happened to Mia. My parents were both alive. Both well.'

Daniel said nothing, but his warm brown eyes never left her face.

'But my dad met someone else. I think he'd always had a "someone else" but this time it was more serious. I came home from school early and found them together, and he threatened me.'

Daniel swore softly.

'I never did tell my mum, but I think she knew. There were huge rows.' Freya smoothed out an imaginary crease in her trousers. 'And my mum's drinking escalated. She used to drink vodka, mainly.'

'Freya . . .'

He said her name like a caress.

'She crashed the car once and my dad hit her. Just that once. I don't think either of them knew I'd seen, but I was watching from the upstairs landing. Mum told me she'd slipped on the stairs.'

'Did anyone else know?'

Freya blinked hard, her eyelashes heavy with unshed tears. 'My parents were great at pretending. That was more important than anything. Eventually my mum didn't even object to Dad bringing his girlfriends back to the house. We just didn't talk about it. And they still did the social rounds together. Everyone thought they were very charming.'

'What about Margaret? Did she know?'

'I don't know. We've never talked about it. Even now. I suspect on some level she must have known, but my dad is very smooth.'

'And you got into a bad crowd?'

'It was a slow journey. Eventually they were the only people who would accept me.'

Daniel looked down at the leather of his shoes. 'So what do you think is happening to Mia?'

'She probably doesn't know why she's doing what she's doing. Inside she'll just feel frightened and lonely.'

His eyes met hers. 'I can't be a mum to her.'

'Just love her unconditionally. Someone once said to me that the only people in your entire life who will ever love you unconditionally are your parents. If you're lucky.'

He was listening. She knew it. His body language had changed.

'A husband or wife will have certain expectations of you. Your children will. But if you're really lucky your parents will love you whatever you do.'

'I love her.'

Freya swallowed. 'I didn't have that. But it's really important. It's that unconditional love which keeps you upright, whatever life throws at you. It's the core that convinces you that you're worth something.'

'Self-esteem?'

'I don't believe Mia would have gone out of her way to have a fight with anyone. There'll be a reason, but no one seems to have asked her.'

Daniel bit the side of his lip.

'I know I hardly know her, but she seems to me to be testing everyone. Pushing as hard as she can to find out how far she can go before she gets rejected.'

'By me?'

'Mainly you, I think. But I don't know that. I just know that if you do reject her you'll have confirmed what she's feared all along. She —' Freya broke off as a waitress brought across their paninis. Both the same, she set them on either side of the table. 'Thank you.'

Daniel leant forward and set his beer glass down on the table. 'I do love her.'

'I know you do.'

He smiled sadly. 'But she doesn't think so. You're right about that.'

Freya picked up her plate and settled it

on her knee, gingerly picking up one half of the panini. 'She hopes you do.' *And it's up to you to convince her.* She stopped short of saying that. There was no need.

'Hell.' Daniel pulled a hand across his face. 'You really don't pull your punches, do you?'

*Not when it mattered.* 'I like her.' *I like you, too.*

She bent her head to take a bite of her panini. He had no idea how rare it was for her to actually like someone. To let down her defences enough to make trusting anyone a possibility. With sudden clarity, she wondered whether she ever had.

'I probably did neglect her when Anna was ill.'

'That's not so surprising, is it?' Freya said quickly.

'I was working long hours in the City, taking time out to go with Anna to her oncology appointments. Days off to sit with her while she had chemo.'

Freya wanted to weep for him. The pain of that time was in his voice. Of course he hadn't thought about Mia. He'd probably been so scared.

'And then she went into remission and we decided to change everything. Move here. Start this business because it was what I'd always wanted to do.' He looked across at her. 'Mia cried because she didn't want to leave her friends in London, but we did it anyway.'

He took a deep breath, forcing out a little bit more. 'Within months of our being here Anna's cancer was back.'

*And she'd died.*

Freya sat in silence.

'I should have taken more time to explain to Mia what was going on.'

Easy to see that now, but at the time Freya was sure it had been an impossible balancing act. She knew a great deal about setting up a business. She knew the long hours — incredibly long — she'd put into the first couple of years of her own company. Daniel must have been stretched beyond capacity. Both in terms of time and emotional strength.

'God, what a mess.' He thrust a hand through his hair in sheer exasperation.

He'd paid her the compliment of not offering her mindless platitudes, and she didn't intend to do that to him, either. It *was* a mess. And the way back would be slow. It might even take years. People were hard to fix.

'Thank you.'

Freya put her panini back down on her

plate. 'For interfering?'

'For caring about Mia enough to try.'

*She cared about them both.*

He looked down at his uneaten panini. 'I'm not so very hungry now.'

'It's nice.'

Daniel picked it up and took a bite. 'As addictions go, it's not a bad one. So, what about you now? Are you still scared?'

*Oh, yes.* His voice was low and quiet, and it seemed to reverberate through her bones. Her yes followed after. She was incredibly scared of what she was beginning to want.

She shrugged. 'I'm twenty-nine, not fifteen.' But the fact was she was still searching for acceptance. Still wanting someone to love her unconditionally and to be proud of everything she'd achieved. And she was beginning to want that someone to be Daniel.

'I don't know that age makes much difference if you don't have that core of self-worth.'

A trio of women came through the archway to the left of them and stopped while they waited for the rest of their party. Freya looked up, more because they were standing close than because she'd remembered to be nervous. There was something vaguely familiar about one of them, but she couldn't be sure until the brunette turned and spoke quietly to her friends.

The slightly plumper of the other two turned to stare directly at her, and Freya cringed.

'It *is*.'

Then there was laughter, and the stupid and ineffectual effort they made to suppress it.

'Stacey!'

Their friend came running. 'I'm sorry, I couldn't find —'

As the group started towards the door Freya looked away, just catching her name as they left.

'Let's go. I've had enough.'

Freya looked across at Daniel, not needing to ask whether he'd heard. She gave him a wry smile. 'I wonder how accurate her account will be.'

'Probably very inaccurate,' he said, picking up his coat. 'By the time she's finished she'll probably have you abducting teenagers and running your own pickpocket syndicate. Let's go.'

When Daniel looked at her she felt precious. *Did that make sense?* No one looked at her the way he did. And it made her feel beautiful. Cared for.

Daniel held the door open. 'My dad once

told me that criticism is only worth listening to if it comes from someone whose opinion you rate.'

'Good advice.'

'Which means I think you can disregard that nonsense. Who the hell do they think they are, anyway?'

She looked back at him and smiled. It didn't matter that the women were still huddled together in the car park as they passed. Or that they would probably be adding two and two and making seventeen. If Daniel didn't care, why should she?

'I'll talk to Mia,' he said as they walked into the auction house forecourt. 'We're going to have more time together over the next little while. Maybe that'll be a good thing that comes out of her being expelled.'

Freya stopped at her car and searched the bottom of her bag for her car keys. 'I'll be here tomorrow and carry on getting your office sorted.'

His hand reached out to touch her arm. Freya looked up.

'Thank you.'

And then he kissed her on the cheek. A gentle touch of his lips on her skin. Freya gripped her keys hard, willing the pain of the metal biting into her soft flesh to prevent her raising a hand to touch where he'd kissed her.

His kiss hadn't been about sex. Or lust. Or any of the things she'd experienced before. It had been liking. It had been gratitude.

And maybe, just maybe, it had been a little about love.

# CHAPTER EIGHT

Daniel hadn't been able to stop thinking about Freya. All morning, just knowing she was there, working away, she'd filled his mind. It was why he'd deliberately come back late. He'd needed to prove to himself he could.

It couldn't be for much longer. The two weeks she'd suggested were already over. He was on borrowed time.

Daniel opened the door to his office, and he could smell her perfume hanging in the air. So faint, but it seemed to surround him. There were traces of Mia, too. Her make-up bag left open on his desk. Some of her GCSE Art work laid out on the desk in the corner.

He walked over and studied it. She'd inherited more than her colouring from Anna. She seemed to be doing something on mermaids. The silhouettes were strong, but the overall effect was rather eerie. Anna

173

would have loved it. She'd have encouraged Mia more than he'd done — or could.

'The girls have gone out,' Bob said, popping his head round the door.

Daniel looked over his shoulder and let the drawing fall back on the desk.

'Freya said to say she'd left you a note. Somewhere by the computer, she said.'

'Here?' He walked over to pick up the folded A4 sheet propped up against the screen.

Bob shrugged. 'Don't know. After that tutor woman left they went out. Said something about a window.' He shrugged again. 'Can't rightly remember.'

Daniel opened the sheet. *Freya's handwriting.* He'd got used to seeing it on scraps of paper. Messages telling him to phone someone or other. Asking him to clarify what some piece of paperwork she'd found was. More often than not with some kind of curlicue or abstract doodle somewhere.

'They've gone up to St Mark's to look at the stained glass window.'

'That was it.'

Bob left and Daniel sat down at his desk, strangely reluctant to get down to any work. The art nouveau mirror which had come in earlier would normally have had him happily researching to see if he could attribute it to Liberty. He did open his notebook, but that was about as far as it went. His mind was elsewhere.

He glanced up at the station clock on the far wall. They'd still be there. He might prefer to think he wanted to join them because he needed to work on his relationship with Mia, but he knew that more than half the pull was Freya.

*The woman he'd been thinking about since the moment he'd woken up this morning.* The woman he'd thought about yesterday. And the day before. And the day before that.

He pushed back his chair and stood up. *Damn it.* There couldn't be any harm in going to join them if Mia was there. However tempted he was, he couldn't kiss her with his daughter watching. The thought of kissing her was beginning to be all consuming.

'You off for lunch?' Bob asked as he passed.

Daniel raked a hand through his hair. 'I'll grab a sandwich. My mobile is on if —'

'If we need you,' the older man finished. 'I've just accepted a whole load of pictures. There's a couple of paintings and some drawings. What do you think?'

'I'll check them out when I get back.' Daniel looked up at a rug which was hanging from a high rail. 'I'm not so sure about that,

175

though.'

'No reserve. We should be able to get it out of here.'

Daniel gave a grunt and then walked back out of the auction house, car keys in hand. He hesitated, and then put them in his coat pocket. If he drove up he might miss them, and St Mark's was barely a mile across the fields.

Daniel followed the hedge round to a narrow stile which marked the entrance to a public right of way. The old church was immediately visible, its grey stone tower dramatic against the stormy skyline. He raised his collar against the sharp wind and lengthened his stride.

He heard Mia before he saw either of them. She was laughing, and he felt a huge weight drop from his shoulders. It was a sound he'd not heard in such a long time. He only hoped she wouldn't freeze up again the minute he appeared.

It didn't matter how often he told himself he had to be the adult in their relationship. That it was better she took her grief and frustration out on him as opposed to other people. It still hurt.

'Dad!'

Freya turned her head to look at him, her hair blowing in the wind. He liked her hair loose and blown about. And he loved it when she smiled. Her sensual mouth curved in a way that sent his libido into the stratosphere.

'You got our note?'

'This window is wicked.'

Daniel looked over at the impressive circular window which had been the object of such devoted fundraising when he'd first arrived in Fellingham. 'Why do you need to look at it?'

'I'm going to draw it. It's going to be a part of a series.' Mia held up her phone. 'I've got some great pictures.'

'Don't forget to take a photo through the arched gate.' Freya said, settling herself on a bench. 'Then we can get back. My ears are frozen.'

Daniel smiled, sitting beside her. 'You need a hat.'

'Too late now. Hurry up, Mia. I've had enough.'

Rather than complain, Mia flicked through the photos she'd already taken and then started off down the path. Daniel watched her until she'd disappeared. 'I didn't know she needed pictures of windows.'

'She didn't. It was something they talked about during today's session, and I remembered this one as being pretty spectacular.

Mia's spotted all kinds of other possibilities. She's really good at all this stuff.'

'Like Anna.'

Freya huddled down in her sheepskin jacket, her hands firmly in her pockets. 'In case she forgets to tell you, she needs to get some more charcoal.'

'Right.'

'And some special kind of pencil. An HB-something. But they're all HBs, aren't they?' Freya turned her head and caught him smiling.

'I suppose I don't need to wait for Mia to finish now you're here —'

'Have you seen inside?' he asked, cutting across her.

'Will the church be open? I didn't think to try. I assumed it would be shut up against vandals.'

'No, this one is kept open. The vicar thinks it's important.' He stood up.

'Shouldn't we wait for Mia?'

'I will. You can go in and look around.'

Freya jumped up. It hadn't even occurred to her that the church would be open. Too long living in London, she supposed.

'Nice boots, by the way.'

She glanced down at her sensible walking boots, and then up into his glinting eyes. 'Fellingham's not exactly the right terrain for my Jimmy Choos. I bought these in Ol-ban at the weekend.'

Freya stepped up into the stone porch and moved to take hold of the heavy iron handle. It twisted easily in her hand. 'It *is* open.'

'Didn't you believe me?'

She glanced back into his teasing eyes and her stomach dropped a few hundred feet. Freya stepped down into the church and the smell of polish and fresh flowers met her like a wave. Thick white candles were set in each of the arched windows, and the blue-grey winter sunlight streamed through the stained glass window behind the altar.

Just beautiful. She wasn't much of a churchgoer, but this place had always felt holy. She loved the solid feeling of perma-nence, and the way the flagstones had been worn down by the hundreds of feet that had walked over them. And she loved the hand-stitched kneelers that were hanging on the back of the pews.

Freya picked up the visitors' book and flicked through it, glancing behind her as the door opened and Daniel stepped inside.

'Mia will come in in a minute.'

'Okay,' she said, turning back to the book in her hand. 'You know, people have come here from Australia and Thailand. And there's quite a few from the States.'

Daniel stood so that he could read over her shoulder. She could feel the warmth of his body. If she turned around she'd almost be in his arms.

'There's a steady stream of tourists who come to trace their family trees. Apparently there was a whole contingent who emigrated from here after industrialisation made life tough in the country.'

Freya traced her finger along 'Randy and Laura Williams' to read their comment. 'They're right about it being a special place. I always thought that.' She shut the book and set it back on the top of the oak table.

Daniel stepped back to allow her to pass. He paused to look along the pews and up towards the altar. 'I've not been here in months.'

'Is Anna buried here?' Freya asked, as the thought occurred to her.

He nodded.

Freya bit her lip, wishing she hadn't asked that question. If she'd paused to think before she spoke she'd have known that it was likely. The Jamesons had always been church, not chapel.

'She was christened here. Confirmed, too.'

*And then buried.* Freya breathed in the comforting smell of polish. It was so incredibly sad.

'Were you christened here?' he asked.

'Oh, yes. My parents had some kind of big formal do with everyone they knew invited.'

'Nice.'

'Daft. They weren't churchgoers, but they dressed up and made promises which meant absolutely nothing to them. Their only purpose was to get nice glossy pictures.'

Freya turned away and started walking down the centre aisle, looking down each row of pews as she went. 'Here it is.' She pulled one of the kneelers off its hook. 'This was my favourite. I used to use it as a cushion when I came here to read. I've no idea why I liked it so much now. Perhaps because it had flowers on it. I don't know.'

She looked round to see Daniel standing facing the altar. His face looked sad. Freya put the kneeler back in place and walked out to join him. 'Does it make you sad to be here?'

'No, not really.'

She paused, and then asked a little hesitantly, 'Were you thinking about Anna's funeral?'

He looked down at her and smiled. 'Am I that easy to read?'

*To her, yes.* She was beginning to find it very easy to sense his moods — and, more amazingly, she cared about them.

'I think pretty much everyone came from the village. The church was crammed full of people. I can't honestly remember who was here and who wasn't. They were just a sea of faces.'

Freya remained silent, watching each change of expression.

'It was good, though. Anna would have liked it. If that makes any sense,' he said, looking down at her. 'And in the end it was a relief for it all to be over. I was so tired.'

Daniel brushed a hand across his face and walked back up the aisle towards the font. Freya's eyes followed him. It all made perfect sense to her. Watching someone you loved suffer was desperately hard. She could imagine wanting it to be over, and then feeling guilty when your wish was granted.

Did Daniel feel like that? Did he *still* feel like that? It explained why he'd not spoken to Mia about Anna as much as he should. It was all so sad.

Freya took another deep breath, loving the sense of peace that seemed to permeate every stone, and looked up at the high vaulted ceiling. She'd like to be buried here. Eventually. There was a certain symmetry to the whole thing. Christened. Married. Buried.

She looked back at Daniel, standing by the doorway and thumbing through a hymnbook he'd picked up off the side. 'Did you get married here?' she asked, walking towards him.

He smiled, his eyes suddenly laughing again. 'You're forgetting Anna was already pregnant with Mia. By the time we did the decent thing she was already seven months gone, and her parents couldn't have coped with a wedding in their village.'

'I must have still been living here,' she said, inconsequentially. 'How old was Anna then?'

'Twenty.'

Freya did a rapid calculation. 'Yes, I was. Fifteen. I was Mia's age now.' She smiled up at him. 'Just think — if you'd married here I'd have come to watch. I was a real wedding groupie.'

'Why?' he asked, holding open the door to the church.

'I liked to see the dresses. I used to sit on the wall over there and watch them all.'

His eyes softened as they looked at her. She'd got absolutely no idea what he was thinking, but it sent a warm shiver coursing through her body.

'It seemed like such a fairy tale. I particularly liked the brides who arrived in a horse-drawn carriage. That seemed so romantic to me. Less so when it rained, of course,' she added with a smile.

'Is that what you'd do?'

'If I got married?'

He nodded.

Freya laughed to hide her sudden embarrassment. 'If I ever trusted anyone enough to make that kind of commitment I'd do the whole thing. I'd want the big white dress, and to wear something borrowed and blue.'

'And carry myrtle?'

He was laughing at her. She knew it from the wicked gleam in his eyes, but suddenly she didn't care. She'd spent so many years hiding behind a tough nothing-can-touch-me exterior when actually she really did want the whole fairy tale.

'I'd do it all. Why not? You only do it once.' She wanted a happy-ever-after with a man who kept his promises. *With a man like Daniel.*

'I'd have thought you'd have chosen an up-market London hotel and given it all a minimalist theme.'

'I'd have a veil and orange blossom. And one of those huge three-tier cakes with icing so thick it can't be cut without snapping. And my groom would wear full morning dress.'

'And if he objects?'

'He's marrying the wrong girl. Weddings should be romantic, don't you think? Or why do it?'

He seemed slightly stunned, as though her answer had been the last thing on earth he'd expected her to say.

It probably was. No one would ever have expected that the girl who'd sat drinking cans of lager in the bus shelter was also a girl who'd drawn ball dresses in her notebook.

'What kind of wedding did you have?'

'A quick registry office do in Hillingdon, where we were living.'

'Oh . . .'

'I know.' He smiled. 'It wasn't at all romantic. To be brutally honest, Anna's parents had ruined any chance of that. They treated her pregnancy like some kind of Greek tragedy.'

'But they love Mia now?'

Daniel hesitated. 'As long as Mia behaves in the way they want. They have very high expectations.' He carefully shut the church door behind him. 'I don't think Anna even had a new dress for our wedding. I can't remember.'

'Daniel!'

He laughed. 'But we did the deed.'

And they'd been happy — until her illness had robbed them of all that.

'Did you stay in Hillingdon?'

'For a few years. Then when I'd started earning better money we moved further into London — to Fulham.'

Freya stopped walking. 'Fulham! That's a *lot* better money. What did you do?'

'I was a trader.'

'On the Stock Exchange?'

'Uh-huh.' Then, his eyes glinting down at her, 'Surprised?'

'Very.' More than surprised. 'That's a hell of a change. City trader to country auctioneer.'

'Huge.' Daniel looked about him. 'No sign of Mia. We'd better go and wait for her back on the bench.'

'Did you always want to be an auctioneer?' Freya asked, following him.

'No. Actually, paintings fascinated me more. If I'd not been quite so money-orientated I'd have headed off for some kind of art-connected thing.'

'Painting?'

He shook his head. 'I'm strictly art appreciation. I've got zero skill when it comes to the creative side. I'd have liked to run my own gallery. Something like that.'

Freya sat down and studied his profile. How *extraordinary.*

'It's how Anna and I got together. We met at an exhibition of Lowry's paintings. They were on loan from the gallery in Manchester —' He stopped. 'What?'

'So where did the auctioneer bit come in?' Freya asked, holding back her hair from the wind.

Daniel crossed his ankles and leant back. 'That was a much later passion. We kitted out our entire first home at an auction, and I just loved it. The smell as much as anything, I think. Mustiness and chip fat. It's a heady combination.'

His sexy eyes invited her to laugh at him, as though he thought it was impossible she'd have any understanding of that.

'I just found it exciting. We'd talked about it, Anna and I. Those kind of "what if" conversations you have.'

*No.* She'd never had a 'what if' conversation, because she'd never been in any relationship where she'd talked of the future. Planning a couple of months ahead had seemed like a bit of a commitment.

Daniel continued, oblivious. 'Anna fancied moving to the South of France and living a self-sufficient lifestyle.'

*Anna!* She really hadn't known her at all.

The woman Daniel had loved was absolutely nothing like the girl she'd imagined her to be.

'Was that a no?'

'My French is appalling, and it seemed like too much of a hand-to-mouth existence to me, so we compromised on my dream. Sold up, cashed in all our investments, and bought the auction house here.'

'Do you regret it?' Freya asked curiously as Mia appeared round the corner.

'Leaving London? Not in the slightest. I'd only ever seen that as a short-term thing. If I was going to have to work I thought I ought to make some money at it.' Her face must have shown her incredulity, because he laughed out loud. 'You look so shocked.'

'Only because people don't *do* that sort of thing! The odd journalist, perhaps. But I reckon that's only so they can write about it.'

'Aren't *you* downshifting? I thought you were having a major life re-adjustment?'

*She was.* She was doing just that. She'd sold up her business and was searching about for something she could pour her heart and soul into. 'Yes, but I wouldn't dream of buying an auction house. That's a real learning curve.'

'Except my uncle is an auctioneer down

in Brighton and my dad is an antiques dealer in Petworth. It was a lot like returning to the family business. Finished?' he asked Mia as she joined them.

'Yeah. I guess.'

'We can come back,' Daniel said, standing up.

'I need to get some charcoal.' Mia lifted the hood of her jacket.

'Freya said. I'll take you to Olban on Saturday.'

Mia's whole stance changed. 'But I need it *now!* I can't start any of this stuff without it.'

It was rather like watching two stags squaring up to each other. Freya could just sense World War Three about to erupt between father and daughter. Daniel was right. Of course he was. Mia was being unreasonable and rude. But she did need that charcoal, and he probably didn't understand quite how important it was to her.

Freya stood up and adjusted her soft pink scarf. 'Would it help if I ran Mia into Olban this afternoon?'

'Cool.'

'Mia, we can't —'

'*Why?*' Mia turned on him like a volcano exploding. 'You always spoil everything. *Always.*' She flung her arms wide and

189

stalked off down the path.

'Mia!'

Freya bit her lip. 'Sorry.'

'That wasn't your fault.' Daniel turned his head to look at her. 'That was a nice offer, but she's got to learn that people can't just drop everything when she wants something.'

He was right. *But . . .*

But Mia was really keen to get started on her drawings — and that was a good thing, wasn't it?

'I won't say anything else to Mia, but I'm happy to take her if it'll help.'

He started to shake his head.

'The sooner she gets her charcoal, the sooner she can start. The busier she is, the less time she'll have for Steve.' Freya fiddled with the end of her scarf, aware that Daniel was looking at her curiously.

'She told you about him?'

Freya nodded.

'You're honoured. I'm not supposed to know.' He answered the unspoken question in her eyes. 'Fellingham isn't a great place to keep secrets. I've been told by at least three or four people. Margaret included. And, yes, I want Mia too busy to go anywhere near him.'

'Is he really bad news?'

'He's nineteen, unemployed, and been in

trouble with the police. What do you think? What's he doing with a fifteen-year-old, anyway?'

Fortunately the question was clearly rhetorical, because Freya didn't fancy giving him the answer that leapt to her mind. She'd inadvertently broken one confidence, and she wasn't about to break another, but he had more to worry about than their age difference. *Did Daniel know his daughter wanted a baby?*

Freya had said what she could, focussed on what a huge commitment it was to have a baby, but she didn't flatter herself Mia had changed her mind. She hadn't thought further than the lovely clothes she could buy it, and she hadn't given any consideration to where the money for them would come from.

There was another reason, too. Unexpressed, but Freya was certain Mia wanted a baby because it would be something that was hers to love.

'Back down on the trip to the art shop. We could stock her up on pencils, paper, pastels . . . She'd love it if you bought her a set of those.' Freya watched indecision pass over his face. 'Tell her I've convinced you I really don't have anything else to do this afternoon.'

'And don't you?'

She pulled out her mobile. 'Nothing that can't be sorted with a phone call.'

*'Hell!'* His hand ripped through his hair. 'I don't like to —'

Freya reached out and touched his arm. Her fingers closed about the waxy fabric of his jacket. 'I'd like to.'

'I seem to spend a lot of time thanking you.'

'You're welcome.'

His eyes seemed to darken, and Freya knew he was thinking of the time he'd kissed her on the cheek.

'Okay. I'll break the good news to Mia on one condition.'

Freya took her hand off his arm, suddenly shy. 'What?'

'Come to supper with us.'

She hadn't expected that. Freya looked up at him, trying to search out whether he was merely being kind or whether he actually wanted her to accept. Since that kiss he seemed to want to keep his distance. He'd been grateful, stopped to talk, but he'd not repeated his invitation to lunch.

'It's not going to be anything fancy, but you deserve a proper thank-you.'

She'd begun to think he was doing the right thing. Helping out in his office, she'd come to see how much a part of this community he was. He was happy here as she'd never been. And she suspected he was still in love with his dead wife. No one could compete against a ghost.

But . . . she wasn't strong enough to turn down the chance to spend time with him. *Before she left.* Where would be the harm in that? 'I'd like that. Thanks.'

# CHAPTER NINE

Freya stopped to unlace her walking boots.

'You don't have to bother with that,' Mia said, dropping her coat into a cupboard and pushing the straining door shut with her hip. 'Dad doesn't care.'

Nevertheless, Freya eased her foot out of the second boot and left the pair carefully by the front door. She'd tried hard during the past three hours not to speculate on what kind of place Daniel would call home, but this was pretty much what she'd expected.

Given his love of antiques, she'd guessed at old, but couldn't imagine him in something too cottagey. For one thing he'd have to perpetually duck under the low doorways. But this was perfect. One of the six late-Victorian semis which lined the road out to Kilbury. The ceilings were high and, if the hallway was anything to go by, the decoration was plain and masculine.

She liked it — although it was a world away from her interior-designed penthouse suite overlooking the River Thames. There, everything was arranged according to Feng Shui principles and nothing was allowed to mar the overall harmony.

But this felt more like a home. The pictures which lined the walls were incredibly eclectic. Colourful brash paintings sat side by side with subtle pencil drawings.

'Dad'll be in the kitchen.'

Freya padded along behind her as Daniel called out, 'Mia?'

'Yeah. We're back.'

And then he came round the kink in the hallway, book in hand. Freya felt her stomach lurch at the sight of him. It was instantaneous. Almost like a reflex action. She seemed to have absolutely no control over it.

'Hi.'

Who'd have thought jeans and a loose open-necked shirt could look so sexy? His feet were bare, too. It seemed a strangely intimate thing to have noticed. Domestic.

'Did you get what you wanted?' he asked his daughter.

Mia's words tumbled over themselves. If Daniel had wanted to distract his daughter's attention away from her boyfriend he couldn't have happened upon a more likely way to do it. Mia was passionate about art. She drooled over sticks of pastels like other girls her age lusted after make-up.

'And Freya said you wouldn't mind if I got all twenty-four colours,' she said, holding up a box of pastels. 'I was going to buy them individually, but this was cheaper.'

Above her head Daniel met Freya's eyes. He said thank you as clearly as if he'd spoken. She let her mouth soften with what she hoped said *you're welcome.*

In fact, she'd genuinely enjoyed the afternoon. Mia was good company. A little spiky, but then she'd have been bored if she hadn't been. And Freya had taken the opportunity to talk about Steve. The baby plan didn't seem to be more than an abstract idea. Which was good.

'I'll put them outside,' Mia said, pushing past her dad.

'I've given her Anna's studio.'

'I bet she loves that.' Freya followed Daniel up the hallway. In all her speculation she'd forgotten that this house had been Anna's home, too. Had she chosen the neutral colour walls? The solid oak floor? Were any of the paintings hers? It didn't seem unlikely that at least one or two would be.

He stepped down into a large family kitchen with hand-painted blue-green cupboards and dark granite worktops. Through a large archway she could see a sitting room which was dominated by an entire wall of books.

It was that kind of house. Large comfortable sofas, kelim rugs, the kind of kitchen that belonged to someone who loved to cook.

'Wine?'

'I can't. I'm driving. Water will be fine.'

Daniel laid the book he'd been reading open on the large wooden table. 'Why don't you leave your car here and collect it tomorrow?'

'I —'

'It's only a fifteen-minute walk to Margaret's, and I'll walk you home later.'

*How tempting was that?* During the afternoon she'd almost managed to convince herself her feelings for Daniel were entirely altruistic, but an invitation like that blew everything out of the water. She wanted to be with him. Wanted to spend time with him. Even though she knew he wasn't looking for a relationship and that she was unlikely to be his choice even if he were.

Wine glasses were hanging on a wooden rack, and he pulled one off and poured in a large quantity of red wine. 'Red or white? There's white in the fridge, if you prefer that.'

'Red's fine.'

Daniel handed her the glass and pulled another goblet off the rack for himself. The wine was more than fine. It was the kind that had a thousand flavours bursting in your mouth and yet the whole was somehow unified. It was the wine of a connoisseur, and if she hadn't known about his London lifestyle she'd have been surprised.

'This is gorgeous.'

He smiled. 'I'm glad you like it. Have a seat,' he said, gesturing at one of the bar stools.

Freya set her wine glass down on the granite work surface and settled herself on one of the high stools. Her stomach was churning over and over. He made her feel so vulnerable. Nervous.

She felt as if she'd got her nose pressed up against the window, looking inside at a life she wanted. And inside her a voice was saying *Please love me; Please want me.*

Her hand closed around the stem of her glass. *Love?* Had she thought that?

Matt had told her she didn't know what love was, and she'd been inclined to believe him. She didn't 'do' love. Ever. It was a cut-off mechanism. The point at which she backed off.

Because deep down she thought love was a con. It was something men said when they wanted to have sex with you. Something her parents had said when they'd wanted to control her behaviour or punish each other.

Twenty-nine years had taught her love was a lie — but Daniel made her want to believe it wasn't. Freya twisted the stem between her fingers.

'You're not a vegetarian, are you?' Daniel asked, his hand on the fridge door.

'No.'

'Good,' he said, pulling out three fillet steaks. 'A bit late to be asking.'

He turned to look at her and she felt her body respond. His eyes seemed to look right into her soul. So often there was that mix of warmth and laughter. He made her feel *liked.*

Not a body. Not a means to an end. Someone he actually enjoyed being with. And she really enjoyed being with him. Could this be what she was looking for? Was this the big life-changing *something* she'd sold her business to give herself time to find? Was Daniel *it?*

*Was she in love?*

And what about him? What was he really

seeing when he looked at her?

Daniel put the first fillet into the hot pan. 'How do you like your steak?'

'Rare.'

'Two rare and one cremated.' He put the other steak fillets into the pan and then leaned over to take a sip of his wine.

Freya sat quietly running the events of the past three weeks in her head. Was being in love like this? Was it an awful churning fear of rejection? Was it a feeling of horrendous uncertainty?

It wasn't like that in books. Heroines were supposed to *know.*

Daniel knew what it was like to be in love. He'd loved Anna. He'd loved her when she'd been tired from the chemo, when her hair had fallen out, when she'd been too ill to really care whether he was there.

*She wanted that kind of love in her life.*

'How much do I owe you?' Daniel asked, with a look over his shoulder.

'Mia has the receipt.'

He nodded and flipped over the steaks with a palette knife. 'I'll get that off her and settle up.'

'Can I do anything?'

Daniel shook his head. 'It's all done bar the steaks.'

Which left her with nothing to do. Freya

took another sip of wine and then let her eyes wander around the kitchen, searching for little touches she could attribute to Anna. Did he still surround himself with things that would remind him of her?

The sad truth was it probably didn't matter whether or not she was in love with Daniel, as he wasn't likely to fall in love with her.

Sophia would have told him about Jack. About the squat, too. Freya took a small sip of wine and watched as Daniel took a saucepan of new potatoes out of the oven, where he'd been keeping them warm. Sophia knew all about them.

What else had he been told about her? Had he picked up on the suggestion she'd overheard the other day that she was a kind of professional girlfriend? That her car was an ex-boyfriend's present for 'services rendered'?

The truth wasn't so bad, but it wasn't so great, either. She'd had three important relationships with three very different men — the one unifying thing being that they'd all cheated on her. She'd bought the car herself, with money that was hers, but that had wrecked her relationship with Matt.

Why would Daniel want her?

He'd been kind. He'd let her work in his

office because he'd thought she'd needed it. Let her grow close to his daughter. Offered her friendship.

But none of that was love.

It was time she left. All the major clearing of her grandma's house had been done. Long done. Even the loft was empty. But she'd stayed.

For Daniel or for Mia she couldn't quite tell. Maybe a little of both. But for how much longer could she let things slide like this?

Maybe what she should take from this experience was that there were nice men out there? And maybe the payment for that knowledge was that she'd been able to do something to help Daniel's relationship with his daughter?

'Penny for them?'

She looked up with a start.

'Your thoughts. You were miles away.' Daniel laid the steaks onto warm plates.

Freya straightened her spine. 'I was. I was thinking about Mia.'

He untwisted a roll of foil and cut slices from chilled butter flavoured with Roquefort cheese, red pepper and black pepper, laying them across the top of the steaks.

'She was brilliant today. Have you heard anything else about whether she can go back to take her exams at Kilbury?'

'That's not going to happen. And, actually, I think it's probably for the best. It would be hard for her to go back now.' He looked up. 'You were right, you know, when you said there'd be a reason she got into that fight. She'd gone into Art that morning and found some of her work damaged. Everything snowballed from that.'

'Her poster for *A Midsummer Night's Dream*.'

'She told you?'

Freya nodded.

'Why didn't you tell me?'

'Mia said she was going to. And that's better, isn't it? She needs to talk to you. I'm not going to be here for ever.'

Daniel stood straight. 'I suppose not,' he said slowly.

*He knew that.* From the very beginning he'd known Freya didn't intend to stay in Fellingham. The very fact she'd come at all was a huge surprise. So why did it bother him so much when she said it aloud?

He'd made the decision to keep his distance. Certain it was the right thing to do. Nothing had changed. Mia still needed all his attention. And Anna . . .

Daniel twisted his wedding ring round. They'd never talked about this. Through all the appointments, the treatment she'd endured because she'd so desperately wanted to live, the days in the hospice, they'd never talked about 'after'. He didn't know what Anna would have felt about him remarrying.

He looked across at Freya as a bright light burst inside his head. Was that the way his mind was working? Was that the reason he wanted to keep his distance?

'This is ready,' he said, moving to pick up the platter with the steaks on it.

'Shall I carry it through?'

'That would be great.'

Freya slid off the stool and walked through into the dining area. He swallowed. His reasons for keeping his distance suddenly didn't seem so clear any more.

'Is it ready?' Mia asked, bursting back into the room.

Daniel lifted the lid off a salad spinner and tipped a selection of salad leaves into a wide bowl. 'On the table. Mia, take the plates across, will you?'

He took the dressing out of the fridge and picked up the bowl of new potatoes.

'Can I have some wine?'

'A little,' Daniel said. 'Get yourself a glass and bring the bottle.'

Freya was standing looking at his bookshelves. 'Is there anything you don't read?' she asked, looking back at him.

He smiled. 'It's probably more of an addiction than Spicy Meatball paninis.'

'That's bad.'

'What about you?' he asked, setting the bowl of new potatoes down on the table. 'Please sit down.'

'Anywhere?'

He nodded. 'To be honest, we rarely eat in here. We usually use the breakfast bar in the kitchen.'

'It's nicer in here,' Mia said. 'How much wine can I have?'

Daniel took the bottle from his daughter's hand and poured her a generous third of a glass. 'Sip it slowly. If you're thirsty you should drink water. In fact, bring a jug of water through, with three glasses.'

He followed Mia back to the kitchen and brought the salad bowl, and the dressing in a separate glass bottle. Freya had settled herself at the table, her hands cradling her wine glass and her eyes sparkling.

'A top chef says you kill your salad within three minutes if you put dressing on it,' Mia said, putting the water jug down in the middle of the table. 'I saw that on the telly yesterday.'

'That's why I've put it in the bottle.'

'Which glasses?' Mia asked, as though he hadn't spoken.

Daniel sat down opposite Freya. 'Use the ones in the top cupboard.'

Mia nodded and went back to fetch them. He couldn't remember the last time Mia had co-operated like this. It was because of Freya. Because she wanted to impress her.

And the truth was he wanted to impress her, too.

He watched as she took another sip of wine. Watched as she let the flavours swirl about her mouth. The tip of her tongue as it licked her bottom lip.

*Hell, but he was so out of his depth here.* He'd been married for such a long time he didn't know how this was done.

'Do you really read Tolstoy in the original Russian?' Freya asked.

Mia returned with the glasses. 'He does. And Russian poetry.'

'I do.' *Was that really boring?* Daniel looked across the table to see what Freya was making of it all.

'*And* he's never failed an exam.'

Her blue eyes turned on him. 'Never?'

Daniel shook his head. ' 'Fraid not.'

'What was your degree in?'

'Pure Maths.'

She pulled a face, exactly as he'd known

she would. Everyone always did. Unless they happened to be a mathematician and got the same buzz from numbers as he did.

'Okay, so that's all my dirty linen out in the open. What are *your* secret passions?' he asked, putting a steak on her plate.

'They're secret.' Freya reached for the salad.

'That's not playing fair.'

'Okay — well, I think I might have developed a similar addiction to Spicy Meatball paninis, because I had another one today in Olban.' She poured dressing over her salad in one easy movement. 'And I love shoes.'

'How many pairs do you own?' Mia asked.

Freya bit the side of her lip. 'You don't want to know. And I've a bit of a thing for handbags. And perfume. And nice lingerie.'

*Please God, she couldn't read his mind.* Daniel concentrated on putting dressing on his own salad.

'And stationery,' she continued, adding a few potatoes to her plate. 'There's nothing better then getting a new notebook. Oh, and I love computers.'

Computers didn't seem to fit with the rest of her list.

'She's done a wicked template for your website, Dad.'

'You don't have to use it,' Freya said, with

a quick look in his direction. 'I was playing about.'

'It's really cool.'

She shrugged. 'I love that sort of thing. I know it bores everyone else, but I find it really satisfying. It's as much about branding as designing great packaging.'

Daniel sat back and listened. With Mia prompting the conversation he really didn't have much to do but sit there and glean as much as he could about her. He learnt that she'd taken three goes to pass her driving test, that her favourite colour was blue, that she'd wanted to keep a pet mouse but her mum wouldn't let her, and that she knew how to make a honey and oat face mask.

And every now and again she would look at him, her face unreadable.

After white chocolate cheesecake they moved through to the sitting room, with its large and comfortable sofas. Mia settled herself on a leather beanbag and he sat opposite Freya, so he could watch her face.

The truth was he absolutely loved seeing Freya in his home. He'd known he would. On some kind of level somewhere that sixth sense had kicked in and he'd known. She seemed to fit.

He loved the way she swirled her red wine in her glass, as though she knew something about what she was drinking. He loved the way she unconsciously pushed back her hair when she was talking. And the way she'd relaxed into his sofa, tucking one foot beneath her.

Daniel leant forward and studied his own wine, swirling it in his goblet. He'd been in love before. He knew how it felt. There had been that moment when he'd looked at Anna and had known they belonged together. It had all been so easy.

He looked across at Freya, laughing at something Mia had said, and knew he was right at the edge of that moment. Standing on the precipice, deciding whether to jump or not. Because that was what it took. That decision to go for it and hope to God she'd be there to meet you.

Would Freya be there to catch him? It was harder this time. He didn't know how you did the dating thing. When did you take a woman to bed for the first time? His wine swirled all kinds of colours red. Had things changed in sixteen years? Did people really just fall into bed with each other a couple of hours after meeting? If so, he was way behind on his game. He'd wanted to make love to her for days.

What would it be like to slip that crocheted tunic off her shoulder? It was practically there anyway. He wanted to kiss the hollow of her shoulderblade. Peel the white T-shirt off and make love to her.

Did Freya want him? Sometimes when she looked at him he thought . . .

It should be so easy, but it wasn't. Daniel looked over at his daughter, her face slightly ruddy from the heat of the open fire. He had Mia to think about. He wasn't free to just take what he wanted.

Mia liked Freya. Was that enough?

And what kind of woman was Freya really? He hardly knew her. She glanced over at him and smiled, her hair a blonde halo around a face that was so beautiful it seemed to shine.

*He knew her.* On some deep, fundamental level he'd always known her. He'd heard the stories, but he *knew* she was as lovely inside as out. As flawed as he was, and sexy beyond belief.

*So, did he jump?*

Mia uncurled herself from the floor cushion. 'I'm going to get some cola. Do you want any, Freya?' Freya held out her half-full wine glass. 'Dad?'

He shook his head. 'I'm good.' Then he watched as she walked down the step into the kitchen. He could hear the sound of the fridge door, the clunk of her glass against the granite.

Freya took a sip of wine. 'I ought to be getting back.' But she leant back again, against the soft cushions of his sofa. 'Trouble is, it's hard to move after eating so much. Have you always cooked?'

'No.' He could happily spend the rest of his life watching her. She was almost feline in the way she curled herself in front of the fire. She looked sleepy. Relaxed. 'I only started when we moved here.'

'When Anna became ill?'

He liked the way she did that, too. There was no pity in her eyes. No awkwardness. She merely wanted to know. And he found he liked talking about Anna. It didn't mean it changed the way he was feeling about Freya. He shook his head. 'When I stopped working City hours.'

'Oh, yes — the City.' Her sexy blue eyes laughed across at him. 'You don't look like a City trader.'

'Not now.'

'But you did? I should have liked to see that.'

Was that the kind of man Freya was attracted to? Did she crave top London restaurants? The fast cars which made no sense in a city so crowded it had to levy a congestion charge? *The lifestyle he'd re-*

*jected?* Was that what she wanted?

'Is there anything you miss about London?' she asked.

'The art galleries. Theatre.' He smiled. 'But even when I lived in London I hardly ever went. I just liked knowing it was so near.'

Freya pulled her top higher on her shoulder, only for it to slip back down. 'I never go, either. Crazy, isn't it?'

'What about you? If you decide to leave London, what will you miss?'

'If I go travelling, you mean?' She uncurled slightly and leant forward to put her wine glass on the low trunk which served as a coffee table. *What would she miss?* It was a hard question.

Freya settled back on the sofa, pulling a cushion onto her knee and hugging it towards her. 'I like the noise outside my bedroom window. Strangely.' She smiled, trying to put words on what she meant. 'Cars. People. The sense of something being about to happen. The buzz of living in a city, I suppose. And I'm very attached to the Starbucks at the end of my road. I like going there for breakfast. And . . .'

She hadn't got a clue what she'd miss, really. She hadn't allowed herself anything that could genuinely be called a 'lifestyle'.

She'd had work. Her *raison d'être.*

She didn't even have the kind of friends who'd be there in times of trouble. Her fault. She'd not made time and space to make any. She'd had colleagues. People whose mortgages depended on her.

And at the end of each long working day she'd known that when she shut the door that was it. She wouldn't speak to another living soul until she went to work the next morning.

'Starbucks?' His voice was incredulous.

She shrugged, her mouth twitching. 'Cappuccino each and every morning. It's my drug of choice.'

'As drugs go, that's not so bad. Have you — ?' And then he stopped abruptly.

Daniel didn't ask a lot of questions. He hadn't asked about her time in London as a teenager. Or anything about Jack. He didn't even know what she'd done for a living.

Maybe he wasn't that interested? But she thought he was. His eyes rested on her too long. Hovered on her mouth as though he were thinking what it would be like to kiss her.

'Drugs?'

'I'm sorry. Rude question.'

'Well, I smoked too many cigarettes. Does that count?' she asked. 'Mainly to annoy my

213

parents, but I didn't much like it. You?'

He shook his head. 'Clean-living guy, me.'

'What's your one vice?'

Daniel held up his glass. 'Really, *really* expensive wine. I think I could easily become a complete wine bore. I'll probably end up going on those wine-tasting tours.'

'That's quite a nice vice. Have you never smoked?'

'And ruin my palette?' he said in mock horror.

'Would it?'

'Uh-huh. Never trust a chef who smokes.' He took his last sip of wine. 'My grandparents on my mum's side were wine merchants from way back, and my parents are real wine buffs. Foodies, too. It was just part and parcel of my childhood.'

'Are they still alive?' she asked, watching the way the light from the fire caught the angles of his face.

'Both of them. They're still in Petworth, running their antiques shop. My sister lives nearby in Pulborough, with her four children.'

'Four?'

'And I've got a brother in Hong Kong who's earning the mega-bucks.'

She liked imagining him against the backdrop of his family. 'Do you see much of them?'

'Less than I like. Richard hardly at all. But when we do get together it's like pulling on an old jumper. Claire is hugely busy with her own family. Since Anna died I've tended to take Mia down to Sussex each Christmas, and we spend a week or so in the summer with my mum and dad.' He placed his hands behind his head and stretched back. 'What did you do this Christmas?'

Freya thought of the ready-made meal she'd bought on her way home from work on Christmas Eve. The pile of romantic comedy DVDs she'd borrowed in case there wasn't much on TV she fancied.

'Margaret was with your dad, wasn't she?'

She nodded. Her grandma did that most years. She called it 'keeping the channels of communication open', and said that it was 'just a day — nothing to get too het up about'.

Christmas dinner with her dad and his new wife was more than Freya could handle.

'This year I spent it at home,' she said carefully. 'I watched too many movies, had too much to eat.'

'By yourself?'

'This year. It is just a day.'

Daniel looked thoughtful. His clever dark eyes seemed to reach in and see too much. He had a habit of doing that.

Freya drained the last of her glass, then looked at her wristwatch. 'It's almost eleven!'

'Is it?'

'I ought to be going.' She stood up and straightened out her crotchet top. 'My grandma is probably waiting up until I'm home safely.'

Daniel stood up. 'I'll walk you down.'

'It's —'

'What's going to happen?' he said, in a voice that brooked no arguing. 'If Margaret is going to be waiting up for you then I'm not having my reputation for "niceness" ruined.'

'I don't think I've been walked home since I turned fifteen.'

'But then you picked very bad friends.'

She couldn't deny that.

'Mia,' he said, walking through to the kitchen. 'I'm just walking down into the village with Freya. I'll be back in about half an hour.'

'Cool.'

Freya rubbed at the goosebumps which had inexplicably appeared on her forearms.

Mia appeared in the doorway. 'Are you

going to work tomorrow?'

'I think so,' she said, with a glance across at Daniel.

At some point she was going to have to stop this. It was fun to pretend for an evening, but it was ultimately pointless. She was going to wind up hurt.

Daniel paused to put the fireguard in front of the fire. 'I'll sort that out when I get back. I've got my mobile on me if you need me, Mia. Okay?'

'Yeah.'

'I'm sorry it's so late. I didn't notice the time,' said Freya.

Mia drained the last of her cola. 'It's not that late.'

'It is for my grandma. She's a strictly bed at ten o'clock kind of woman. I bet she's a got-to-lock-up-safely kind of one, too.' Freya walked down the hallway and picked up her walking boots, quickly slipping her feet in and lacing them up.

Mia followed, setting her empty glass down on the hall table. 'Here's your jacket.' She pulled back the curtain and swore. 'It's snowing.'

Freya walked over to stand beside her. The ground was more frost than snow, but the sky was full of the kind of soft snowflakes that might settle.

'The forecast was snow,' Daniel remarked, coming up behind them. 'I didn't quite believe it, but they're spot-on.'

She was such a child. Snow would always be magical to her. Freya laced up her book, wrapped her pink scarf round her neck and pulled on the pair of suede leather gloves she kept in the pocket of her sheepskin jacket.

Outside the air was crisp, rather than freezing, and the ground was crunchy beneath her boots. The wind had dropped from earlier, which made it feel far less cold. And the night sky was a clear, dark black and dotted with tiny white stars.

'This kind of weather always makes me feel like I've stepped into a Victorian Christmas card.' Thick heavy snowflakes fell on her hair and quickly mottled her jacket. Freya glanced over at Daniel, walking beside her. 'I suppose *you* think about how difficult it's going to make the roads tomorrow.'

He smiled. 'I am that boring.'

For one moment she wondered whether she'd offended him, but his smile reassured her. 'I hope it settles.'

'I think it will. It's cold enough.'

They turned into Ellis Road and walked on down into Rope Lane. Freya just felt happy. Beneath a sky like this, she felt as though anything were possible.

'I hope my grandma isn't sitting up for me. I shall feel so guilty.'

'I bet she isn't.' Daniel's arm lightly brushed against hers.

They rounded the final bend into the top end of Fellingham's narrow High Street. Her grandma's house was positioned sideways, so it wasn't until they'd scrunched their way into the driveway that Freya could see the sitting room light was off.

'She must have gone to bed,' she said with a glance up at him.

'And left the hall and landing lights on for you?'

'Yes.'

Daniel waited while she searched for her keys. Freya felt unbelievably flustered. Why did keys always fall to the innermost corner of a handbag? She pulled them free and refastened her bag. 'I had a really lovely time with Mia this afternoon.'

'Thank you for taking her.' His eyes were on her lips.

Freya struggled to breathe. Every atom in her body was begging him to kiss her. She moistened her lips with the tip of her tongue. 'And dinner was wonderful, too.'

'You're welcome.'

'I've not had such a nice evening for —'

'Freya.' Her name on his lips was half-ache, half-moan.

Her eyes flicked up to his. She must have communicated something, because he ripped off his gloves and his hands were warm on her cold cheeks. He held her so that he could look deep into her eyes, very gently, and then he moved to kiss her.

That first brush of his lips against hers sent shock waves soaring down her veins. And then his tongue flicked against her bottom lip and her mouth opened to receive him. This was what she'd wanted since the first day she'd met him.

Her chest felt tight and her breath was coming in ragged gasps. This was so much more than any kiss she'd ever received. There was something desperate about it. Almost forbidden. And so entirely perfect.

Daniel drew back and rested his forehead on hers while he steadied his breathing. His hands remained cradling her face, his thumbs moving along her cheekbones.

'I've been thinking about that for such a long time,' he said huskily.

'Me, too.'

He groaned and kissed her again. Hard and fast. 'I need to get back to Mia.'

'Yes.'

His lips moved against hers, his tongue

thrusting into her mouth and tangling with her tongue. Freya's hands slipped up his back and held him close. He smelt of night-time air and cold, and he tasted of the wine they'd shared.

'Will you be in tomorrow?'

Freya nodded silently, and he kissed her again.

'I don't want to go,' he said, moving back to look into her eyes.

She didn't want him to. It would have been the easiest, most natural thing in the world to take him upstairs and make love to him — but that wasn't going to happen tonight.

His thumb moved once more against her cheekbone. 'This is crazy.'

'It's going to need thought,' she said, smiling up into eyes that seemed to offer everything she'd ever wanted. He made her feel so safe. So desired. So *loved*.

'Hmm,' he agreed, closing the gap between them for one last kiss. It stretched on for the sexiest length of time. 'You'd better go in. If Margaret is watching from behind the curtains you're going to have some explaining to do.'

Freya gave a gurgle of laughter. 'That'll be your reputation besmirched.' She put her key into the lock and opened the front door.

'Goodnight.'

'Night.' He held onto the pillar of the porch.

Freya walked through to the sitting room, without turning on the light, and watched as Daniel walked slowly away.

*He'd kissed her. Really kissed her.* She could still taste him on her lips. And that felt absolutely incredible.

# CHAPTER TEN

Daniel's arms slipped round her waist and she turned in his arms. 'You've had three messages and one wrong number,' Freya said against his mouth as he came close to kiss her.

His face was cold, and his hands even more so, but she forgot that as he kissed her. She let her fingers slide up into his hair and gave it a firm tug. 'Two need you to call back really urgently.'

She could feel him smile against her mouth. 'I'm too busy.'

'Not for a couple of Victorian stuffed bird scenes, surely?'

He stood back, his face everything she'd hoped. 'Really?'

Freya couldn't stop the laughter. 'No, not really. I just know how much you love taxidermy.'

His hands were quick to pull her closer. She loved the way his hands cradled her face. It made her feel as though he were really concentrating on kissing *her.* This time his lips were warm and oh-so-sensuous.

She could feel heat pooling in her abdomen and spreading out like a sunburst. Freya let her hand fist against his shirt as he flicked his tongue between her lips.

Vaguely, very vaguely, she heard voices approaching. 'Daniel.'

He stood straight. 'I hear it.'

Freya hurried round to the other side of the desk and pulled out the notepad where she'd written his messages. Daniel raked a hand through his hair, turning as the office door opened.

From the look on Bob's face they'd probably fooled no one. 'Dan, I've got someone out here who'd like a word.'

'Right,' he said, with a quick glance over his shoulder. 'I'll make those calls in a minute.'

Freya bit her lip to stop the laughter bubbling out uncontrollably. She'd never been this happy. Even when she'd been spending long hours building her own business.

She put the notepad back down on the table and went through to the kitchenette to put on the kettle. She loved him. Trusted him. *Enough to tell him about the money?*

That was more difficult. There'd been a

couple of times over the past week when she'd almost told him. It wasn't that she didn't want to — it was more a case of lack of opportunity. She wanted to tell him in the right way.

Freya poured boiling water into a couple of mugs. Matt's voice sat in her head. It was as she'd always thought. You couldn't isolate the present from the past. Even though Daniel was a very different kind of man, she still carried the scars from that relationship into this one.

'Any good?' she asked, as she came back into the office and found him sitting at his desk.

'Could be. He's a Hornby train collector whose wife has decided it's her or it.'

Freya passed him his coffee. 'Your messages are on the first page of that notepad.'

He glanced at them briefly and then looked back up at her. 'They can wait. I want to talk to you.'

His voice had taken on an unfamiliar edge. Freya let her hands slide round the warmth of her mug and held it comfortingly against her lips.

'Don't look like that,' he said, pulling her towards him.

Freya set the mug down on the desk and reached out to smooth back the hair from his forehead. One week in, she didn't feel so very confident. 'What, then?'

'I want you to come with me to a reception at Kilbury Manor next week.'

Her hand stilled.

'Fun though this is, we're going to have to go public some time.'

Fear licked through her. She liked it like this. As soon as they went public the real world would intrude upon them. 'What about Mia?'

'Freya, we can't keep doing this. It feels like something furtive, and there's absolutely no need.' Daniel linked his fingers through hers and pulled her closer. 'You told me you were tired of letting other people judge you for something that happened twelve years ago. Let's lance it. Let's let them get all their gossiping out of the way in one fell swoop.'

His thumb moved against the palm of her hand.

'What's the worst they can do?'

*They could spoil this.* It was so bright and new she didn't want to let anyone into their relationship yet. Even Mia. She didn't want his daughter to put any doubts about it in his mind. It was too fragile a relationship. Too much pressure and it might snap.

'What happens at Kilbury Manor?'

'It's just a charity fundraiser organised by

Lady Harrold in aid of the local hospital. She's done it every year for the last five years.'

Freya chewed the side of her mouth nervously. 'Did you go with Anna?'

'Yes.' Daniel stood up and brushed her hair off her face, looking closely into her eyes. 'I was married to Anna. She's part of who I am.'

'I know that. It's only that people are going to think I'm a poor exchange.'

Daniel let his hands slide across her shoulders and down her arms, gathering her hands loosely in his. 'You're not an exchange. Anna died. And I've found you.'

Which only meant that if Anna had been alive he wouldn't have looked at her. Which, of course, she wanted. If he'd been the kind of man to wander she wouldn't have been interested in him. But . . .

She couldn't even straighten it all out in her own head, let alone explain it to anyone else. She was just feeling neurotic, that was all. Nervous.

'What happens at the fundraiser?'

'The great and the good of the Downland Villages gather together. It's very formal, slightly dull, but it's the most obvious place to make a statement about you and me.'

*You and me.*

'When is it?'

'Next Saturday.'

'Can I think about it?'

Daniel shook his head. 'No. We need to get tickets.'

His thumb continued to move against the palm of her hand, but other than that he didn't move. Just waited. *Why* did they have to go public? It was perfect the way it was.

Well, perfect except that they had nowhere they could guarantee they'd be alone. And that they were lying to Mia by omission. The logical part of her brain knew that he was right. This was one of those forks in the road. They could either decide to go forward with this relationship or they were going to have to decide not to.

'Okay.' The single word was wrung from her.

Daniel leant forward and kissed her. 'It'll be fine.'

*Fine.* Daniel didn't know what he was talking about. There was nothing fine about any of this. Freya put on the last layer of lipstick and turned to go downstairs. She'd been in Fellingham almost six weeks now, and people were still talking about her. Yesterday yet another conversation had stopped abruptly the minute she'd walked into the farm shop.

'What do you think?' she asked, standing before her grandma and twisting round so she could see the low scooped back. Back in London she'd decided it was the most classic of all the evening dresses she possessed, but now she was wondering whether she should have just popped into Olban and bought something a little more restrained.

'You look lovely.'

'It's not too much?'

'It looks lovely,' Margaret repeated, looking up from her crossword. 'And it'll shock half the people there. As well you know,' she added.

'Too much?'

Margaret set her pencil down on her paper. 'Freya, you must have been to this type of thing before. They're inclined to be stuffy. Everyone stands about making mindless conversation and juggling silly little bites of food they probably wouldn't eat if they knew what they were. The point is, if you want Daniel you're going to have to go. And there's no point in pretending you're some kind of twinset and pearls woman, because you're not. You've always dressed to stand out from the crowd. And to shock.'

Margaret looked back down at her crossword and Freya fingered the single diamond nestling at her throat. It was the first time her grandma had let on that she knew about her fledging relationship with Daniel.

The elderly woman's mouth twitched into a smile. 'Of course I know. I saw you last week. And if Daniel kissed you as thoroughly as it looked from where I was standing, I'd say you had something worth the odd barb or two.'

'Will the Jamesons be there?'

'I imagine so.' The doorbell rang. 'Just do it.'

*Just do it.*

'And take your key. I doubt I'll be up when you get back.'

Freya leant forward and kissed her grandma's cheek.

'You do look lovely. And I'm so proud of you,' she added softly.

Tears smarted at the back of Freya's eyes. She blinked them away as she lifted her velvet wrap from the back of the chair and wrapped it round her shoulders. Then she picked up her clutch bag and went to open the door, letting in a blast of cold air.

Daniel looked quite different in his dinner jacket. She could imagine him as a City trader so much more easily than she could when he was dressed casually. He looked sharp, and scarily sexy.

'You look beautiful.'

Freya cleared her throat in an effort to dislodge the lump of fear that had settled there. 'You look fairly good yourself.'

He smiled and reached for her free hand. It felt better with her hand tucked in his. He led her towards the waiting taxi, watching while she settled herself in the rear passenger seat before shutting the door and walking round to join her.

'Have you told Mia we're dating?' Freya asked, turning her head to look at him as he sat beside her.

Daniel shook his head. 'It wasn't that kind of a night. Mia wants to go to a party.'

'Where?'

'She doesn't know. And she doesn't know what time she'll be back. What time it starts.'

Freya bit down on her lip. Daniel's voice was thick with a mixture of exasperation and frustration.

'And Steve will be driving her there.'

'What did you do?'

Daniel leant back on the headrest and turned to look at her. 'Shouted quite a bit.'

'Oh.'

'*God*, Freya, I don't know what I'm doing wrong with her.'

Freya slid her hand in his and squeezed his fingers. 'You're doing great. Just keep doing great.'

'So I've got poor Melinda Tilling from next door to come and sit in. I couldn't risk leaving her alone tonight. So, no, I didn't tell her anything about us.'

'Good decision.'

Daniel cracked a smile. 'I feel like I've gone two rounds with Mike Tyson.'

Kilbury seemed to loom quickly. The taxi driver took the second junction and followed the winding road out towards Kilbury Manor.

'Have you been here before?'

Freya looked out of the window at the predominantly Tudor-built house. 'No. Though I think my parents did a couple of times. What would that have been for?'

'Before my time,' Daniel said, with a shake of his head.

The taxi came to a stop, and the driver got out to open Freya's door. She swivelled round on her seat and climbed out with an easy flick of her legs.

Now she was actually here she felt strangely calm. Her grandma was right. She *did* know how these events worked. It was all about posturing, really. You just had to hold you head up high and look as though you were extremely comfortable.

Daniel appeared to *be* comfortable. His

hand hovered at the small of her back and he steered her towards the heavy oak door which was standing open at the back of the central courtyard.

'Dan! Hi!'

He spun round, and Freya turned to look at the man who'd hailed him. Cleanshaven, with hair slicked back, he wasn't someone she recognised.

'Hi.' The two men shook hands, and then Daniel stepped back. 'This is Freya Anthony.'

She fixed a smile to her face and held out her hand.

'Freya, this is Ben Taylor.'

'Hello.'

If she'd needed any confirmation that she looked good, Ben's eyes provided it. They took on that lascivious gleam men's eyes often held around her.

Daniel's hand moved to touch the small of her back again. It was both protective and possessive. Freya glanced up at him. A muscle pulsed in his cheek, and she knew he was completely aware of the other man's interest.

'Do men always react like that around you?' he asked quietly as they walked away.

'Not usually after they've talked to me a bit.'

Daniel gave a crack of laughter. 'You *are* very frightening up close.'

The room was a heavy mass of people. She'd instinctively tensed, but relaxed when she saw how easy it would be to hide from anyone she particularly wished to. The fear that she'd have to stand and talk with Professor Jameson and his wife receded.

'There's a makeshift cloakroom set up in the next room. Shall I take your wrap?'

Freya let it slip from her shoulders, the velvet slithering across bare skin. 'Thank you.'

'I'll be back in a minute.'

Kilbury Manor was exquisitely beautiful. Lord and Lady Harrold had filled the hall with exquisite flowers in shades of cream and white. Most impressive was the enormous fireplace right at the centre of the hall. It was blackened with age and a glorious fire had been lit in it. Perfect on a cold February night.

'Okay?'

Freya turned at the sound of Daniel's voice. Actually, she was. There was nothing here she couldn't cope with. Waitresses skilfully moved among the guests with trays of canapés and glasses of wine.

'I'm fine.'

'Shall we go further in?'

Freya nodded and led the way down the length of the hall. Only once did she think she'd been recognised, although that might have been simply on account of her dress. In London terms, Fellingham was a very conservative place.

'Where is Lady Harrold?'

Daniel nodded over towards a grey haired woman in a simple velvet dress. 'Talking to the Mayor and his wife. Lord Harrold doesn't seem to be here. Perhaps we passed him in the Great Hall.' He stopped one of the waitresses and took a glass of white wine. 'White or red?'

'White's fine. I'm happy with either.'

Daniel handed her the glass, noticing for the first time the narrow bangle she wore on her wrist. Everything about Freya was exquisitely understated. Her dark pink dress was deceptively simple. It looked like a silk sheath until she turned around. The back scooped low across her back, held in place by two criss-crossed straps.

*Sexy* wasn't the word to describe it. Every move she made had the fabric shimmering. So much so he could barely keep his hands off her. She carefully picked a tiny new potato topped with dill herring from a passing tray and bit it in half.

'This is nice —'

'And who do we have here?' Major Alling-ham interrupted, thrusting his body between them. 'I don't think we've met, have we, m'dear?'

Freya held up the other half of her canapé as though to ward him off. Or perhaps it was simply to show she didn't have a hand with which to take the one the Major was offering. 'I don't believe so.'

'We need to put that right, then. I'm Major Allingham. Arthur. And you're?'

'Freya Anthony.'

'Are you, now?'

Not by so much of a flicker did she show any kind of reaction. She merely took a sip of wine.

'You're the gal who ran off with that musician boy. Been hearing a fair bit about you. Simon!' The Major summoned one of his friends. 'This is the gal they've all been talking about.'

Simon, mid to late sixties, immediately came over. 'We were wondering when we were going to get a sight of you. I knew your father, of course. And your mother. Very highly strung was Christine.'

'What do you think you're doing?' a familiar voice hissed at Daniel's shoulder.

Daniel swung round to look down at his sister-in-law, elegant as ever in black, her dark auburn hair pinned up in a high chignon.

'Sophy! I was wondering if you'd be here tonight.'

'You knew damn well I'd be here.' She took him by the arm and led him slightly away from where Freya was still imprisoned by the Major and his friend. 'Why have you brought Freya here?'

'Why not?'

*'Why not?'* Sophy repeated, almost spluttering in indignation. He'd never seen her quite so agitated before. 'I've told you what she's like.'

'You don't know her.'

'I know her a damn sight better than you do.' She forced herself to calm down by taking a deep breath of air. 'And look at what's she's wearing. It's so inappropriate. What would Anna have thought?'

'Anna's dead.'

He'd spoken calmly, but his words had exactly the effect he'd intended. Sophy's head snapped round to look at him and her green eyes narrowed. 'Yes, she is. But,' she said, quite deliberately, 'her daughter doesn't need that kind of influence in her life.'

'What kind?'

'Look at her,' Sophy said, nodding back in

Freya's direction.

Since he'd last looked she'd been surrounded by — presumably — a couple more of the Major's friends. Much longer and he would really need to go and rescue her.

'She's always been like that.'

'Like what?'

'Always behaved like a slut.' It was an ugly word, and it hung between them like a slap.

Daniel set his wine glass down on a nearby side table, and then he stepped in very close to his sister-in-law. 'I don't know what happened between you and Freya when you were younger. I don't even know what Anna thought about her. She never mentioned her, which would suggest she wasn't a very significant figure in her childhood. But I do know that much of what's being circulated in the village is coming from you, and I'd like it to stop.'

Sophy smiled. There'd been moments during her marriage to Russell when Daniel had felt incredibly sorry for his brother-in-law. Her smile seemed to conceal real malice.

'Dan, I haven't had to say a thing. Everyone knew Freya was the easiest girl in our year.'

Daniel found his hands had balled into fists.

Sophy spun round on her high-heeled shoes and slipped past him. 'Freya,' she murmured as she moved by her.

He watched Freya's long earrings swing as she looked round to see who had called her name. He felt a surge of protectiveness. He so often felt that around her — although there was no doubt she was more than capable of taking care of herself.

'Excuse me, Major,' he said, cutting through. 'I need to borrow my date, if I may?'

'Nicely saved,' Freya said moments later, looking up at him with rich humour in her eyes.

'Why does Sophy hate you so much?'

The expression in Freya's eyes changed. They became guarded, as though she were waiting to be hurt. 'Shouldn't you be asking her?' She took another sip of wine.

'I'm asking you.'

She gave a faint shrug, as though she were resigned. 'I don't honestly know. Not really. Except that boys liked me and I think she was jealous.' Freya looked across the room towards Sophia, who was leaning in towards a handsome man in his midthirties. 'I'm fairly sure she started some rumours about me, and they kind of took hold.'

'Freya —'

'They weren't true — but when does that make any difference to rumours? And I told you I didn't go out of my way to make people like me. In a way, I think I kind of enjoyed the reputation because my parents hated it so much.'

'But you *did* run away with someone?'

For the first time Freya's eyes sparked with anger. If he could have bitten back the question he would have, but he so wanted to know. Curiosity had been building inside him.

'That's common knowledge. His name was Jack. And he was twenty-three and a drummer. He was absolutely everything my dad hated — which made him incredibly attractive.

'And he told me he loved me, and that was exactly what I wanted to hear. I thought everything would be just fine if we could get away from Fellingham. Jack knew people who could put us up, but what he didn't tell me was that it was a very unpleasant squat in South London.

'I thought we were going to play house — maybe have a baby, build some kind of future together — but Jack wanted to party. And when I wasn't so interested in that scene he quickly found someone who was. Is that everything you want to know?'

'Frey—'

She held up a hand to hold him off. 'Don't. This was your idea. You knew I didn't want to do this, and I'm *damned* if I like having to explain myself to you here.'

'She's Anna's sister.'

The look she shot him was full of contempt. 'Right. She's Anna's sister. So we believe everything she says, do we?'

'Frey—'

But she'd swung away, easily cutting a swathe through the room. Daniel raked a hand through his hair. If Sophy had meant to cause trouble she'd certainly succeeded. A quick glance in her direction suggested that she might have meant to do just that.

He swore silently and then went after Freya. He couldn't see her and so walked back through to the Grand Hall, checking each alcove in case she'd taken sanctuary in one of them.

Then he spotted a sudden flash of dusky pink and headed in that direction — in time to see her stopped by a tall man who then kissed her on both cheeks.

'I can't believe you're here.'

Daniel went to stand beside her.

'I was born here,' Freya answered the man tonelessly.

'What? Kilbury?'

She shook her head. 'Fellingham.'

The other man swore. 'I'm from Olban. Blimey, it's a small world. And who's this?'

'Ross, this is Daniel Ramsay. Daniel — Ross Kestleman.'

The introduction meant absolutely nothing to him, but Daniel went through the motions. 'Nice to meet you.'

'I can't believe Freya's been hiding herself here. I've been trying to call you to congratulate you on your mega-millions. How much did you sell for?'

Freya named a figure which made Daniel's head swim.

'Actually, Ross, I was on the point of leaving. I'll ring you when I'm back in London.'

Oblivious to the tension, he said, 'Great.' And then he kissed her again on the cheek.

Without looking in Daniel's direction, Freya headed towards the makeshift cloakroom. Then, as though she'd thought through what she was doing, she stopped. 'Do I need a ticket to collect my wrap?'

Daniel pulled out a pink slip with the number fifty-nine on it and handed it across. 'What was that about?'

'Ross and I dated for a while.'

He quietly registered that.

'And the money?'

Freya stepped forward and picked up her

wrap from the teenager who'd been given that particular job. 'Is there a phone I can use to call a taxi?'

Mutely, Daniel handed her his phone. She took it, but held it loosely in her hand.

'You owned your own company,' he stated quietly, as so many pieces of information fell into place. Her clothes, her car, her expectation that things would happen quickly and in the way she wanted.

'And now I've sold it.'

'Why?'

'Because I was bored.'

Her answer snapped back as though she wasn't taking time to think about anything she was saying.

'And now you're worth millions.'

'Funny, isn't it? The school drop-out has made good.'

Daniel didn't find it at all funny. There was too much information coming at him, too quickly, but he knew it wasn't remotely funny.

She was rich. Incredibly so. She had the kind of money which made pretty much anything a possibility. She could do all the travelling she wanted, stay in the best hotels. She could start a new business. Invest the money and do absolutely nothing for the rest of her life.

*So what on earth could he offer her which would make sharing his life attractive?*

The answer came back with resounding clarity — absolutely nothing.

# CHAPTER ELEVEN

Freya stood holding Daniel's phone. She should have told him. As she watched the expressions pass over his face she wished more and more that she had.

'I told you I was between jobs,' she said defensively.

'Yes, you did.'

'You never asked me where I'd worked.'

'Was there any reason why you didn't tell me?'

She'd hurt him. Every line of his body indicated that. And his eyes looked at her with an expression which ripped through her.

Freya moistened her lips. 'Most of the men I meet are more interested in my money than me.'

He drew a shaky hand through his hair. 'And you thought I was like that?'

'I didn't know you. When I first met you I thought you were married. You still wear your wedding ring.'

Daniel looked down at the gold band on the third finger of his left hand. 'And later?'

'I didn't think it mattered.' The phone in her hand rang shrilly. Mutely, she handed it across to him.

Everything was spoilt. She'd known it would be once they let other people into their world.

She watched as he struggled to get a good enough reception to hear what was being said. He moved further away, and then came back towards her as he ended the call. 'It was Melinda. Mia's slipped out.'

His voice was without any expression at all.

Daniel pressed a couple of numbers and asked for a taxi to come out to fetch them as soon as was possible. 'Ten minutes,' he said, slipping his phone back into his inside pocket. 'I've no idea where she is. All I can do is sit about at home, waiting for her to come back.'

'Did she say anything else about this party? Who was holding it?'

Daniel shook his head. 'Only that they were friends of Steve's.'

'Well, that's a start.' Freya chewed at the side of her nails. She was sure Mia had mentioned something, but it hadn't made a lot of sense and she couldn't remember. 'Steve lives on the Wentworth Estate, doesn't he?'

'Yes.'

'Let's start there. If there's a party going on in any of the houses we're going to find it easily.' She pulled her wrap closer round her body. 'Let's wait nearer the door.'

'I'll kill her.'

'You can't do that until you find her. Have you tried ringing her mobile?'

Daniel swore, and pulled his phone out of his pocket, hitting a couple of keys. 'It's switched off.'

'It was worth a try.'

The taxi came more quickly than expected. Daniel was out in the courtyard and had the door open almost before the driver had pulled to a stop. 'I'm going home to pick up my car. I've only had half a glass of wine, so I'm fine to drive. Do you want me to drop you off at Margaret's first?'

Freya shook her head. 'I'd rather come with you, if that's okay?'

He nodded. She wished she felt she could reach out to touch him, comfort him. But she didn't feel she could. It was as though a sheet of glass had been put in between them.

'I'll get this,' she said, when the taxi pulled up outside his home. 'You get your car keys.'

'Fine.'

She pulled out a crisp twenty-pound note and handed it to the driver, watching as Daniel ran up the drive. He was out again seconds later, and was sitting in the driver's seat with the engine running by the time she came over to join him. Freya slid into the passenger seat. 'Did Melinda have anything else to say?'

'Just that she's sorry.' Daniel pulled the estate car away from the kerb and headed straight for the edge of the village.

The Wentworth Estate was more run-down than Freya remembered. 'Hang on a minute,' she said suddenly. 'Let's ask at the corner shop. They usually know if anything is happening round and about.'

'Where is it?'

'Left at the next mini-roundabout.'

But as they approached it was clear the newsagents had closed.

'We'll just have to drive about a bit.'

Daniel turned the car round in a small overgrown car park and headed back the way he'd come.

'Slow down a second,' Freya said, catching sight of someone she vaguely recognised. She wound down the window. 'Muriel?'

'Freya? Is that you?'

Jack's mum hadn't changed so very much

in twelve years. 'Do you know of any parties going on tonight? We're looking for a fifteen-year-old who shouldn't be there.'

Muriel opened her handbag and pulled out a packet of cigarettes. 'There's a big one going on at the Farmans' place. You know — opposite the Plough?'

Freya frowned. 'Bill Farman's?'

'Well, he's dead now, but his sons stayed on there. Carl and Steve.'

Beside her, she heard Daniel set the car in gear. 'Thanks, Muriel.'

'You're welcome, love. Give us a call some time. It'd be good to hear how you're getting on.'

Freya gave a wave and then wound up the window as Daniel moved the car away.

'Where's the Plough?'

'Turn back the way we've come. The easiest way is to go back out onto the main road and come back into the estate through the other way. It's on that big looping road that goes round the back of the estate.'

'Okay.' His fingers clutched at the steering wheel. 'How do you know Muriel?'

'She's Jack's mum. She's brilliant. She brought up seven children by herself with absolutely no money. And when she found out Jack had left me she rang a couple of friends and got me a bedsit to tide me over.'

'She didn't think she ought to persuade you to come home?'

Freya looked across at him. 'I wasn't ever going to do that.' Then, 'Here you go. Take the first turning and follow the road round.'

Daniel did what she said, and before they'd gone a couple of hundred yards they saw the house where the party was happening. People milled about outside, drinking. Despite the cold, the windows were wide-open and there was loud music blaring out.

'She wouldn't be here?'

'Why not?'

'Why would she?'

Freya felt for the door handle. 'If she's got muddled up with the Farman brothers or any of their friends you need to get her out.' She slammed the passenger door shut.

It was only when someone grabbed at her stole that she remembered what she was wearing. Freya felt a moment's panic, and then experience kicked in. 'Is Mia here? About my height, red hair, fifteen?'

The youth took a swig of his beer. 'Came with Steve?'

'That's her,' Daniel said, coming to stand beside her.

'She's inside.' His words were slurred but he turned round and shouted, 'Mia!'

'It's okay — we'll find her,' Daniel said quickly.

They walked quickly up the overgrown path and straight in through the open front door. The music was deafening. So loud the beat seemed to hurt her heart. Freya pointed upstairs, and then did her best to indicate that Daniel should search the downstairs rooms.

She picked up the edges of her dress and hurried upstairs. Far too many of the rooms had the doors to them firmly shut. From the sound of the bathroom she heard the unmistakable sound of someone being violently sick.

'Mia?' She tapped firmly on the first bedroom door. 'Mia?'

A girl came up the stairs with a bottle of wine in her hand. 'Is that the young girl?'

Freya nodded.

'Red hair?'

'Yes.'

'She's locked herself in the toilet. Get her out. We're all dying for a pee.'

Freya sent up an urgent prayer of thanks and went to stand outside the door the girl had pointed at. 'Mia? It's Freya. Open the door.'

'Freya?'

'Yes. Open the door. I've come to take you home.'

There was the sound of a bolt being pushed back, and then Mia's tear-stained face peered through the crack. The minute she saw Freya she burst into tears, long streaks of mascara running down her face.

'Hey — come on, honey. Let's get you out of here.'

'I want to go home.'

'I know. Your dad is downstairs.'

'Dad?'

Freya pushed back Mia's hair from her face. 'Looking for you. Come on.' She took Mia by the hand and led her down the stairs.

From the other end of the hall Daniel spotted them. He lifted his hand in a wave, and Freya pointed at the door.

'How did you know where to find me?'

'You're forgetting this is where I used to hang out.' She almost couldn't believe it herself. It made it all the more incredible that her parents hadn't exerted themselves to stop her.

But they hadn't. And if it hadn't been for Muriel she'd have been a good deal worse off. Certainly hungrier, because Muriel had often put a plate of chips in front of her.

Daniel came up behind them and pulled Mia into his arms.

'Dad, I'm sorry.'

'What were you *doing?*'

'I know. I'm really sorry. I didn't think it would be like this.' Tears were coursing down her face.

'Are you okay?' Daniel held Mia away from him and searched her face.

'I just want to go home.'

He pulled the car keys from his pocket.

'Come on,' Freya said, tucking Mia into her arm.

Mia clutched at her velvet wrap. 'I'm sorry I spoilt your evening.'

'It wasn't that much fun anyway. I'm just glad you're safe,' she said, opening the back door. 'You get in and sit next to your dad.'

Mia shook her head and climbed into the back seat. Freya made a snap decision and climbed in beside her. She folded Mia against her and held her tight, placing a light kiss on the top of her hair. 'We've got you. You're safe.'

Daniel looked over his shoulder. 'You need to do up your seat belts.'

Freya helped Mia click the middle seat belt into position and then fumbled for her own. As soon as she was settled Mia curved in towards her once more. Freya gently stroked her hair and murmured words she hoped were comforting.

She looked up and caught Daniel's eyes in the rearview mirror, watching them. He'd been lucky tonight. He had to know that. The Farman family had always been synonymous with trouble. She didn't want to let her mind stray into what might have happened to Mia.

It was far better to concentrate on the fact that she was safe and unharmed. Though it wasn't surprising that Daniel's face had an ashen tone, and that he was incredibly quiet all the way back home.

He helped Mia out of the car. 'Let's get you inside and tucked up in bed.'

Freya stood back to let them pass, quietly shutting the front door as they started to climb the stairs. 'Shall I make a cup of tea or something?'

He nodded, but she wasn't entirely sure he'd heard her. She slipped off her stilettos and padded down to the kitchen, holding her long dress off the floor.

*This had been Anna's house.* As always, the thought popped into her head. It was *her* daughter upstairs. *Her* husband.

She dropped her wrap on one of the stools and placed her clutch bag on the work surface. She couldn't do this. She couldn't step into Anna's life.

And Daniel probably didn't want her to.

He was attracted to her. She knew that. But she wasn't sure that was enough. He'd need to love her enough to let her challenge the decisions he'd made with Anna.

She couldn't see that happening. This house was part of that. Being in Fellingham was. The auction house.

Freya set the kettle on to boil and calmly went about making tea. Had Anna chosen the kettle? The kitchen cupboards? Perhaps she'd even chosen them with her sister?

There was no sound from upstairs. No sign of Daniel reappearing, either. He was staying with Mia. And that was as it should be.

She wouldn't love Daniel as much as she did if he didn't put his child first. Freya poured tea into one mug and sat down to drink it, all the time listening for the first sounds that he might be about to join her.

It seemed interminable. Perhaps she should have called a taxi the minute she arrived? Maybe she should have asked him to take a small detour and drop her off at her grandma's?

At last she heard his footsteps on the stairs. Daniel walked slowly into the kitchen.

'Tea is in the pot. It's probably still okay.'

Daniel walked over and lifted the lid. What he saw must have been all right, because he poured himself a mug of tea.

'Is she okay?'

'She is now.' He pulled a tired hand through his hair. 'This Steve tried to persuade her to have sex with him.'

Freya's hands tightened on her mug.

'When she told him she didn't want to he left her to find someone who would.'

'Good for her for saying no.'

Daniel looked over at her.

'That can't have been easy.' She finished off her tea. 'Look, I'll call a cab to get me home. I just wanted to know she was fine before I left.'

'I can drive —'

'No, you need to be with Mia.' She swallowed, knowing what she was going to say next, but wishing she didn't feel she had to. 'And I think it's time I went back to London.'

Daniel slipped off his dinner jacket and laid it carefully across the breakfast bar. There must have been a part of her which had been hoping he'd say no, because pain ripped through her.

So strange — because she was taking control of this. It was time. And it was her decision. Except it wasn't. Daniel spread his hand out across his dinner jacket and she caught sight of his wedding ring.

*Anna's ring.*

'Anna's family are never going to be happy about me playing any part in Mia's life, are they? And she needs them.' She picked up her handbag. 'And she needs your undivided attention right now. My staying here is only going to make things more difficult.'

'That's it?'

Freya tried for a nonchalance she was far from feeling. 'We always knew this was going to be difficult. And I just think this is the time. Before it all gets horribly complicated . . .'

'You're going back to London?'

Freya nodded. 'I don't belong here. I never have.' She pulled in air. 'Maybe if we'd met in London . . . ? If you'd not been married to Anna . . . ?' She forced a smile and then shrugged. 'All a bit academic, really. I need to use your phone to call a cab.'

'I'll take you.' He left his jacket on the side and picked up his car keys. 'Mia's asleep. It's fine.'

*This was it.* Freya could feel the tears building up behind her eyes. She'd finished it. The one really lovely relationship she'd ever had was over.

He hadn't questioned her decision. Hadn't protested at all. Wrong place. Wrong time.

257

They walked out to the car in silence. The engine, when he turned the key, seemed over-loud. She was aware of every movement he made. His small adjustment to the rearview mirror. His leg as he changed gear.

'Thank you for your help tonight.'

Freya managed a hint of a smile. 'Give Mia my love.'

'I will. Of course.'

In no time at all he'd swung the car into Margaret's drive and pulled to a gentle stop. His hands moved on the steering wheel. 'I'll call you —'

'Don't!' Freya turned in her seat to look at him. 'Let's make this a clean break. You've got things you need to do, and I'd only make them difficult.'

He swallowed hard and then nodded.

Freya pulled her front door key out of her bag and then let herself out of the car. *Not much further and she could cry. One foot in front of the other.*

Even before she'd got her key in the lock Daniel had driven away.

'I shall miss you,' Margaret said, watching as Freya zipped the last things into her case.

'I'll be back.' She looked up and smiled. 'Have that hip operation and you can come up to London and stay with me.'

'What about your travelling?'

Freya shrugged. 'I don't know that I want to do that any more. I'm going to have to think about things.'

She was going to have to think about a lot of things. Aimlessly wandering about the world didn't hold any appeal any more. But neither did spending all her time in an office. Or being a lady of leisure. Maybe she ought to think about doing something for runaway teenagers?

'Why don't you ring him?' her grandma asked softly.

'No.'

'Don't you want to know how Mia is?'

Of course she did. But she couldn't phone. She had to believe things were going to be just fine for Mia from now on. For both of them.

And he could have phoned her if he'd wanted to. Except he knew she was right. And if she was right, she might as well experience the pain of loss now. She lifted her case off the bed.

'That's it. All done.' Freya leant over to give her grandma a tight hug. 'You don't need to come down.'

Margaret clutched at the apricot-coloured counterpane covering the bed and heaved herself to her feet. She stumbled painfully over to the window and pulled back the net curtain. 'Are you sure it's not going to be icy? Your car is covered with frost.'

'All the major roads are gritted. I'll be absolutely fine.'

She let the curtain fall and turned to look at her granddaughter. 'You drive safely — do you hear?'

Freya walked over and wrapped her arms tightly round her grandma. 'I always do. I'll go and get some of that ice off my car, and then I'll be back up to get my bag.'

Her grandma nodded and Freya ran down the stairs, stopping to put on her walking boots and throw on her sheepskin jacket.

She'd feel better when she was on her way. She'd always been like this. Once a decision was made she needed to get on with it. It was rather like pulling off a plaster.

The wind was icy cold. Freya pulled a face and paused long enough to do up her jacket before reaching into the glove department to pull out a plastic scraper. She set about de-icing the passenger window, shards of ice falling across her fingers.

She heard the approach of a car but didn't look up until it started to come into the driveway. *What the — ?*

Freya stopped what she was doing and watched, mystified, as Daniel brought his car in close up against her bumper. She pushed back the hair from her eyes.

'What are you doing?' she asked as he climbed out.

'Blocking you in. I thought we could make it a kind of family tradition.'

She frowned.

'Making it impossible for you not to listen to what I want to say.'

'We said everything last night.'

Daniel shook his head. 'No. You said everything last night. I just stood there too *damn* confused to know what was happening. But this is the morning after the night before, and I have some things to say.'

He walked up close to her — and stopped. His eyes were warm and full of emotion. 'You know, you talked a lot of rubbish last night.'

'Wh— ?'

And then he kissed her. There was a moment when shock held Freya still, but it was only a moment. His lips were too persuasive. His tongue coaxed her response. She felt her hands move to hold him closer, her mouth open to him.

'I love the taste of you,' he said, pulling back. 'I don't think I'm ever going to get enough of that.' His eyes held a new energy, as though the fact she'd kissed him back had given him confidence. 'You'd better shut that door or Margaret will be losing all her heat.'

'Dan—'

He laughed and ran over to shut the front door himself.

'I haven't got my key!'

'I expect Margaret will let you back in later. Come,' he said, reaching for her hand. 'I've got something to say to you, and I want to say it in a particular place.'

Freya held back as uncertainty swamped her.

'You might as well come with me, because you're not going to get your car out unless you do,' he said, his dark eyes glinting down at her.

'Wh-where's Mia?'

'I'll tell you where she is in a bit, but she's great. Come.'

This time she let him take her hand, and he pulled her out of the drive and along the High Street. 'Daniel, where are we going?'

'Up to St Mark's.'

'Why?' She stopped. 'Daniel!'

He laughed. 'You just can't cope with not being in control, can you? But you're going to have to trust me.'

'My grandma won't know what's happened to me.'

'I think she'll have a pretty good idea when she sees my car blocking yours in. You know,' he said conversationally, 'that car of yours really bothered me.'

She started to feel a spurt of irritation. As though he sensed that, Daniel held her hand a little bit tighter.

'I've only just figured out why. Last night when I was thinking about you. *Us.* I've been incredibly slow to realise what Sophy's been doing. She just let it slip that it was the kind of thing you might choose to take away from a failed relationship and every time I looked at your car I wondered what he'd been like. Why you'd left him.'

'I bought the car.'

Daniel smiled. 'So I gather.'

'And Matt left me.'

'Hmm. Yes, well, we'll develop that part of the conversation later. Except to say he was an idiot. And I'm really glad he did, because if he hadn't you wouldn't have ever looked at me.'

Freya felt as though she'd stepped into a movie. One of those beautiful romantic ones where everything ended exactly as you wanted.

'And Sophy didn't just tell *me* about her theory. She dropped it around. By the time she'd told a few people it had become fact, and then it kind of spread,' he said, in an echo of what she'd told him before. 'She's quite good at that kind of subtle innuendo, isn't she? She carefully planted the idea that you always went for men with money. That spread, too. I don't think anyone stopped to question it.'

'Dan—'

'Shh. I haven't finished, and if you interrupt me I'm going to lose the thread of what I want to say because it's all really complicated.' He turned into Church Lane and walked briskly towards St Mark's. 'I'd just never realised quite how insidious remarks like that can be. Even though I've never rated Sophy's judgement, the things she said about you became lodged somewhere.'

'It doesn't matter.'

'It *does* matter. It's not fair.'

Daniel looked down at her with an expression which made her heart turn over.

'And she's certainly not right. After you'd gone last night I sat there and started to unpick it all. I've always known Sophy is inclined to be possessive. She was of Anna. And by extension she is of Mia. I know the last thing in the world she'd ever want is for me to introduce someone else into Mia's life. You are her worst nightmare. I don't know why that is. But she started undermining you from the moment she heard you were coming back to the village.'

Freya stopped. 'Daniel, this isn't just about Sophia and what she says about me. It's bigger than that. It's the whole thing. It's Mia. And Anna. And the fact you chose to live near her family. And —'

'I know. Just hear me out.'

She paused, and then nodded. She had no choice. She was blocked in. But the truth was she'd have listened anyway. Beside her Daniel had tensed, as though he were uncertain of the next thing he wanted to say.

He pushed open the gate that led into the graveyard which surrounded St Mark's, and purposefully led her to a white gravestone.

*Anna Ramsay. Loved and still loved.*

Freya read the inscription. It only told her what she already knew. Daniel had been in love with his wife. Would always love her.

Daniel moved to touch the headstone. 'You know, Anna was very lovely,' he said, without turning round, 'but hopelessly squashed by her family. You know the Professor. He's a very . . . *strong* personality.'

He was domineering and fairly unlikeable.

'As a child she was probably as unhappy as you. She just handled it differently. She tried to please everyone. Particularly her parents. And the Professor values success above all else, so Anna aimed to be the best. She worked hard to get top marks, top grades.'

Freya chewed at her bottom lip.

There was silence for a moment, and then Daniel turned. 'You didn't like her, did you?' he asked, with eyes that were incredibly soft.

His question pulled an honest answer from her. 'I didn't know her. But I really didn't like Sophia, and I transferred lots of that to her elder sister. I hated the way she always got the prizes and everyone said how perfect she was.'

Daniel touched her face, his thumb moving to stroke across her lips. 'You'd have mystified her. Never in a million years would Anna have spent her time in the kind of place we found Mia in yesterday. But she wasn't like Sophy, either. She wasn't a judgmental person. Incredibly accepting, in fact.'

His smile twisted. 'Which is kind of how we ended up in Fellingham. She never did see how controlling Sophy was. She was inclined to take what people said at face value. And she was brave. Really brave. Do you know, she told Mia that she'd always be her mother but that she really hoped I'd find someone who would be a mum to her? Mia told me that last night. I thought she'd feel I was being disloyal to her mum's memory if I fell in love with someone else. So I kept wearing Anna's ring, as though that would somehow make her feel safe.'

He held out his left hand, with a white band clearly visible where his wedding ring had been. 'Mia's got them both now. She's going to get them melted down into some kind of a necklace.'

Freya didn't know that tears had started to fall down her face until Daniel moved to brush them away, his fingers lightly wiping them.

'Don't cry. I don't want you to cry.'

She gave a kind of half-cry, half-hiccup, and then she was tightly wrapped in his arms. Arms which held her so close. She rested her cheek on his chest, feeling the roughness of his wax jacket and his soft kiss on the top of her head.

After a moment he pulled away and looked down into her face. 'You know I haven't finished, don't you?'

Freya brushed her hand across her face and nodded.

'Come over here.'

He led her to a bench immediately to the

right of the main door which looked out across Fellingham. 'Anna and I never talked about after she'd gone. We just lived in the moment. And for the most part I never imagined I'd want to marry again.'

Freya's breath caught in her throat. It was painful to listen to him. She was so full of hope and yet so full of fear. Did he mean he was thinking about remarrying now?

He smiled. 'It hurt too much. The whole thing. Loving and losing it all seemed so pointless.' His voice deepened. 'But then I met you, and I wanted you like I've never wanted anyone before. You kind of blew me away. And I didn't know whether I was coming or going.

'On the one hand I had Mia messing up at school, and on the other I had Sophy dropping little vials of poison in my ear. I decided you were just one complication too many. But then I found I was falling for you anyway — and I felt so guilty.'

She knew this. All of this. Freya looked down at her hands, gripped tightly in her lap. All of that was why she needed to go. She didn't want to make his life difficult.

'Freya, I'm not good at this. The last time I proposed to a woman I said something like, "So we'd better get married, then".'

Daniel looked down at his feet and out

across Fellingham. 'The thing is I love you. I love you so much it hurts.'

Freya stared at him, unbelieving.

His smile faltered. 'I'm scared of losing you. And I'm jealous as hell of the men you've shared part of your life with. I know I've picked a lifestyle you probably wouldn't want to live. And there's nothing I can ever give you that you couldn't buy several times over for yourself. But —' he turned to look directly into her blue eyes '— I love you, and I want to spend the rest of my life loving you.'

'You do?' Her words came out as a hoarse whisper.

'If that means I need to fold up the auction business, then that's what I'll do. If I have to follow after you as you explore Australia, I'll do that too.'

Her head was spinning. 'What about Mia?'

'Mia's definitely in favour.' Daniel stood up. 'Come.'

Freya put her hand in his and let him lead her down the steps into the old church.

Mia immediately stood up. 'Did she say yes?'

'I'd say it's all still hanging in the balance,' Daniel said, releasing Freya's hand. 'We want you, Freya. Part of our lives. Part of our family.'

She felt as though she were only just coming alive. Happiness was spreading out like a sunburst.

Freya looked at Mia. 'Really? You want to share your dad with me?'

The teenager nodded, her young face pinched with concentration.

Daniel moved. He reached out and interlaced his fingers with hers. 'Marry me? Let's change what we need to change to make this work. Let's just do it. Let's make a commitment and spend the rest of our lives making it work.'

Freya looked down at their hands, and then up into his eyes. 'I love you.'

With sudden energy Daniel moved to cradle her face. 'Is that a yes?'

'It's a yes.'

She heard Mia's laugh, and then she was only aware of Daniel's lips on hers. Warm and loving.

'Really a yes?' he said, pulling back so he could look in her eyes.

'Yes.' Laughter bubbled to the surface.

Daniel looked up and round at his daughter. 'I'm glad that's over. I've never done anything so hard in my life!' He held out his arm for Mia to come and join them. 'Let's go home and make some plans.'

She liked the sound of that. Particularly

the 'home' bit. It didn't really matter what they decided, as long as they were together.

'What would you have done if I'd already left for London?' Freya asked.

'Followed you.' Daniel looked down at her, his eyes creating a private world that was just the two of them. 'You are my world. The light after a very dark night. I love you, and I will love you until the day I die.'

# EPILOGUE

*'Something old, something new, something borrowed and something blue,'* Margaret said firmly.

Freya stroked the long lace dress she'd chosen to wear over an oyster silk shift. Simple and — hopefully — stunning. When it had actually come to choosing her wedding dress she'd decided she didn't want to go with her childhood dream of dressing in a meringue.

'This is new.'

'And the garter's blue,' Mia added.

Freya smiled at her grandma. 'And you've given me your old veil.'

'*Given.* So you will need something borrowed,' she said stoutly. 'It's bad luck if you don't have something borrowed.'

'I don't believe in luck.' Freya reached out for the white rose she was going to wear in her hair. 'Mia, will you put this in for me?' Mia came closer and set the rose in the centre of the veil. 'Thanks. How do I look?'

'Beautiful.'

'You need something borrowed.'

Mia looked uncertain for a moment. 'How about this?' She lifted up the pendant she'd had made from her parents' wedding rings. It was beautiful. Delicate and twisting.

'You'd lend me that?'

She unclipped it and handed it over. Freya's eyes filled with tears, and she reached out and hugged Mia hard. 'I love you, you know.'

Mia laughed. 'That's your job. You're my mum.'

'Just don't start crying, you two,' Margaret said, pulling herself out of the chair, 'or you'll make your mascara run. I think I hear my car.'

Freya picked up her hand-tied bouquet of white roses and helped her grandma out of the door.

'You ought to put a penny in your shoe,' she said as a parting shot. 'That's for wealth.'

'I'm not going to be happy if she's organised for a chimney sweep to come and kiss me,' Freya murmured to Mia as her grandma's car drove the short distance to St Mark's.

Mia was looking in the other direction and

laughed. 'Dad said he'd done this.'

Freya turned to look as a pretty horse drawn carriage appeared round the corner. The tears she'd managed to control earlier threatened to spill out over her cheeks. 'When did he do it?'

'Last week. He said it was your dream when you were my age. You've got to admit it's pretty cool.'

Freya took the hand of the man who'd jumped down to help her into the carriage. 'What would he have done if it had been raining?'

Mia was helped in beside her. 'They bring a different carriage. This is so high.' She settled her bouquet on her lap. 'Do you wish your dad was giving you away?'

'I'd rather be with you.' Freya reached out and squeezed Mia's hand. 'And I'm probably too old to be given away.'

'Rubbish!' Mia laughed.

'Mr Ramsay asked me to give you this,' the driver said, handing Freya a single red rose.

She reached out and took it, unwinding the piece of paper wrapped around the stem.

'What does it say?'

Freya held it out. ' "Hurry up!" '

The carriage lurched forward and Freya felt as though she'd wandered into a movie.

After days of rain even the sun had come out to bless her. She could smell the hedgerow, and the fresh clean scent of an English summer day.

St Mark's Church was as beautiful as it had always been. Solid, permanent and loved. She had wondered whether Daniel would prefer to be married somewhere else, somewhere that didn't hold sad memories for him, but he'd said it held happy memories, too.

Freya smiled and tucked the red rose into her white bouquet before being helped out of the carriage.

'You can't do that,' Mia objected, pointing at the red rose. 'It spoils the theme.'

'It's romantic.'

Mia didn't look convinced, but she let it go. 'Ready?'

Freya nodded.

'Then let's go find Dad.'

The huge door was held open, and Freya stepped down into the church. St Mark's had been decorated to within an inch of its life. Her grandma's flower circle had been let loose, and the scent was overwhelming. Music from the old organ filled her ears, but all she was really aware of was Daniel.

Not even her parents' complicated seating arrangements had the power to distract her.

Just Daniel. Tall, dark and handsome, as all heroes should be.

He turned to watch as she walked down the aisle. And then he winked before taking her hand. 'You took your time,' he whispered softly.

'Did you think I wasn't coming?'

His eyes hovered on her lips. 'That's why I insisted on you having Mia with you.'

'Ah.'

He led her up to the altar and leaned in close one last time before the service began. 'Happy Birthday. May all your wishes come true.'

At that moment, Freya wasn't sure she had a wish left that hadn't.

# ABOUT THE AUTHOR

**Natasha Oakley** told everyone at her elementary school that she wanted to be an author when she grew up. Her plan was to stay at home and have her mom bring her coffee at regular intervals — a drink she didn't like then. The coffee addiction became reality, and the love of storytelling stayed with her. A professional actress, Natasha began writing when her fifth child started to sleep through the night. Born in London, she now lives in Bedfordshire with her husband and young family. When not writing or needed for "crowd control," she loves to escape to antiques fairs and auctions. Find out more about Natasha and her books on her Web site, www.natasha oakley.com.

The employees of Thorndike Press hope you have enjoyed this Large Print book. All our Thorndike, Wheeler, and Kennebec Large Print titles are designed for easy reading, and all our books are made to last. Other Thorndike Press Large Print books are available at your library, through selected bookstores, or directly from us.

For information about titles, please call:
(800) 223-1244

or visit our Web site at:
http://gale.cengage.com/thorndike

To share your comments, please write:
Publisher
Thorndike Press
295 Kennedy Memorial Drive
Waterville, ME 04901